A VIEW TO A KILL

A Bird Shifter Novella

MANDY M. ROTH

King of Prey Series

King of Prey
A View to a Kill
Master of the Hunt
Rise of the King
Prince of Pleasure
Prince of Flight

Blurb

A View to a Kill
King of Prey Series Book Two

A trained assassin…a man even the deadliest of warriors fear. To cross him is foolish. To steal his heart is pure madness.

Sachin, head advisor to the king of the Accipitridae realm, has been forced to put his trips to Earth on hold. He's not been honest with himself or King Kabril about his need to visit the primitive planet. The king thinks him to be a womanizer, out to bed as many human females as possible.

In truth, a woman he should have been

able to woo with little to no effort—his mate—has found someone else to fill that void in her life. She wasn't supposed to be on Earth. She wasn't supposed to be human. And she sure the hell wasn't supposed to agree to marry another man while Sachin was away.

Sachin must make a choice, give up the one woman he knows to be his true mate and let her live in ignorant bliss of what walks among her people, or fight for what's his, taking it at all costs. A trained assassin…a man even the deadliest of warriors fear. To cross him is foolish. To steal his heart is pure madness.

Dedication

To my readers. Thank you for being awesome!

Chapter One

EARTH...

Sachin soared high in the air, satisfied after a night of hard sex with three human women. They practically threw themselves at him, as most women in this realm did. They were an itch he liked very much to scratch, even against the orders of his king and best friend, Kabril.

Kabril warned of the dangers of entering the human realm too much. There was a time in human history that his kind, the *Buteos Regalis*, and others like them were thought of as mythical creatures who would steal away with livestock and small children. The stories were absurd. A horse was too heavy to fly with, and why should he bother himself with something like that when he had only to return to the castle to a feast, already prepared. And what purpose would Sachin have with a child? They were noisy, at least from what he remembered. Accipitridae, the realm he called home, had not had a child born to it for hundreds of cycles. No one was sure as to why, but whispers of a prophecy involving the king spread like wildfire. He had to laugh at the idea of the king settling down to be with only one woman.

Sachin couldn't fathom giving up his wicked ways to tether himself to one female for all his life. Eternity was a long time to sleep with the same woman. He shuddered at the thought.

Sachin dipped lower in his flight over the semi-wooded lands on his way to the nearest portal to Accipitridae.

"No!" The cry pierced the night. It was off in the distance but Sachin's super-natural hearing offered him the ability to pick up on it. He scanned the area, trying to locate the source. A blast from a gun, a weapon the humans seemed to favor, went off. Another scream followed. Sachin zeroed in on the location and launched into a dive. He would worry later about humans seeing him in partially shifted form. He was part hawk, part man and they would never understand.

"Come out, come out, wherever you are," a male voice came from the distance.

Sachin neared the spot of the disturbance and spotted a middle-aged man with a rifle in his hands, stalking something or someone. The man pushed greasy strands of hair from his face as he stared around, his eyes crazed. His nose was bulbous and nearly as red as his bloodshot eyes.

"Where are you, you little bitch?" the man spat.

The tiniest of whimpers caught Sachin's attention. He landed silently several feet behind the man—the stench of alcohol and evil evident. It curled Sachin's stomach. He drew his wings back into himself, shifting into his full human form.

He stepped softly, making no sound as he advanced on the drunkard.

A gasp caught Sachin's attention, pulling it to the right. He spotted a figure, huddled in the fetal position. Upon closer inspection, Sachin realized the figure was female and covered in blood. The fierce need to protect her at all costs consumed him. He channeled the rage he felt at the thought of the female having been harmed towards the armed man. Killing him would be a sweet victory.

The man was walking in the other direction, unable to see the female's hiding spot. Sachin motioned to her and then put a finger to his lips to indicate the need for silence. She nodded, shaking so much her teeth chattered.

Sachin bent his head, narrowing his silver gaze. He stepped closer and touched the man's shoulder. He spun, firing the weapon as he did. Using his forearm, Sachin knocked the barrel of the gun away and the shot went wide. The man stared up at him, his eyes wide with fear.

"Who— Where did you come from?"

A tingle of satisfaction at instilling fear in him ran through Sachin. "You dared to touch the woman?"

"Woman?" The man's lips curled into a sinister smile. "Paige ain't no woman."

"She's my woman," Sachin said.

Stunned by his own claim, Sachin blinked, giving the man time to point the rifle at him. He fired and the shot struck Sachin in the shoulder, creating a large, gaping hole. White-hot pain radiated through him. He knocked the man away, sending him hurtling into the air. The man hit a tree and slid to the ground where he lay motionless.

Sachin twisted, his gaze snapping to the female still huddled near a tree. He cupped the wound on his shoulder with one hand. His immortality afforded him the ability to heal rapidly. Even so, the spray from the shells had done considerable damage. The healers in his realm would need to cleanse the wound before it could be allowed to fully heal over.

The woman near the tree needed his help now. Her brown eyes held shock and her shaking was worse. Sachin approached and she cried out, trying to make herself smaller.

He stilled and looked down at himself. Blood dripped freely from his right arm and he cursed himself for not thinking to shield her mind from seeing the events unfolding. Wiping his hand on his pants, he thought back to his landing when his wings had been full. Had she seen him?

"D-don't…don't…hurt me," she stammered.

The idea sickened him. "I mean you no harm."

Moonlight streaked through the tree-tops, casting its soft rays over her hair. If his judgment was correct, she had auburn hair. Her skin was pale, creamy and currently marred with the start of bruises. He wanted to revive the man and kill him again for daring to harm her.

Calming himself, Sachin took a step forward and bent, going to one knee. There was so much blood on her. Sachin wasn't sure how she was alive. "Where are you hurt?"

"Not my blood," she said, her voice low. Their gazes collided and his chest tightened. She was breathtaking, even in her current state of disarray. "My mother."

"What about her?" Sachin reached out tentatively, worried she'd scream or pull away. She didn't, and he began to check her over for signs of injury. Aside from the bruises, he found none.

She scrambled to him, tossing her arms around his waist, nearly causing him to lose his balance. "It's her blood. He… Hank killed her."

Her pain sliced through Sachin. He stroked her hair and held her close, sensing how very young she was. His guess was that she was in her late teens. She clung to him, sobbing openly. Never one who was known for comforting women, Sachin was at a loss as to what to do. He did what felt natural. He kissed the top of her head, ignoring the biting pain and the limited use of his right arm. She weighed practically nothing.

He held her until her crying stopped

and she fell silent. The steady, rhythmic sound of her breathing indicated she was asleep. It was for the best. He allowed his wings to form and lifted her high into the air, already knowing where he would take her—the ranch near the portal. The one run by an older woman who took in troubled teens.

He flew, covering the distance in record time. Upon landing, he quickly shifted into human form and carried the young female to the front door. He tapped it with his foot and waited. A woman he'd seen often enough when flying overhead opened the door. Sachin expected her to question why a man she did not know was holding an unconscious woman on her doorstep. She didn't.

She offered a soft smile and stepped back, opening the door wide. "You can lay her on the sofa."

Sachin did.

"How bad is she hurt?"

Confused, Sachin stared at the older woman, wondering why she was so composed. "The blood is not hers. It is her mother's."

"Is Tandy dead?" the woman asked.

Unsure, he shrugged. "I know not who Tandy is."

"Tandy is Paige's mother." The woman bent near the sofa. "This here is Paige. She helps me tend the horses on her summer breaks." She stood. "Where are my manners? I'm Sarah, in case you forgot."

Forgot?

Sarah smiled. "I met you when I was a little girl. You swooped out of the sky and plucked me out of the ravine I'd fallen into. You told me I was dreaming and that you weren't real. Either I'm dreaming again, or you're real."

Sachin glanced around nervously. He wanted only to have the young female cared for and to be gone from the human realm. Already too much had happened. He would have a lot of explaining to do when he returned to his realm.

Sarah waved a hand in the air. "Your secret is safe with me. I didn't tell anyone about the bird-man when I was little. I'm sure the hell not going to start now."

"You will watch over her?" He stared at Paige, not wanting to leave her, but he'd already exposed himself too much to the humans.

"I'll call the police and the doctor. What about Hank?"

"Hank?"

Sarah nodded. "Her mother's boyfriend. The man I'm sure is responsible for this."

"He is dead." Sachin wasn't a hundred percent sure because he'd not taken the time to verify the man was dead, but it would be difficult to survive being thrown into a tree by a supernatural.

"By your hand?" Sarah held no accusation in her voice.

"Yes."

A faint nod came from her. "Good."

Chapter Two

EARTH, THREE YEARS LATER...

"Paige?"

Paige glanced at Sarah and waved, letting the woman know she was fine. The look on Sarah's face was one of concern. She didn't want to worry Sarah. "He'll come."

"I'm sure he would if he could, Paige, but maybe he's tied up with something."

Sarah was right. Sachin led a busy life, always stopping by for a few days and then disappearing for weeks, sometimes months. It was hard to believe it had been three years since she'd first met him. Her memories of that night were fuzzy and that was most likely for the best. She knew Sachin was the one who'd gotten her help after her mother's death. Her dreams were becoming more vivid, revealing more and more of the events of that dark night. Fantasy seemed to blend with reality, making her dream of Sachin with huge brown wings.

"Want to come in for some supper?" Sarah asked. "Sachin knows where the front door is. If he shows, he'll join us."

Paige clutched the amber pendant he'd given her on his last visit. It warmed in her palm as it always did when she thought of him. "He'll come."

Sarah's eyes crinkled with mirth. "You're a stubborn one, aren't you? Come in if it gets too chilly."

"I will. I promise."

Sarah was so good to her, taking her in when Paige had no place else to go. She'd become a surrogate grandmother of sorts, giving Paige a guiding hand, something she'd never had in her life before. When her mother had been alive, she'd spent her time drinking and doing drugs with her endless line of boyfriends, not mothering

Paige. The last few years had opened Paige's eyes to what a family could be like and she was eternally grateful for Sarah's unconditional love and trust.

The front door closed, taking with it the light from the living room. Paige sat in the dark, sneaking peeks towards the sky, certain the man she'd come to love would indeed sweep down and whisk her away.

Stop living in a fairy tale.

The pendant heated more, making it hard to hold comfortably.

"There you are," Sachin said, walking around the corner of the house.

Paige looked for signs of a car, but like always, she found none. He certainly had odd ways of arriving. None of that mattered. He was here and that was what was important. She stood, suddenly embarrassed by how dressed up she was. Normally, when Sachin came for a visit, he helped her tend to the horses and they laughed, talking about everything and nothing at all. She had something different in mind tonight. It was her twenty-first birthday and she wanted to celebrate.

Sarah had prepared a birthday feast and Paige wanted to head into town shortly after, hopefully with Sachin by her side.

She was on break from school and lonely. It wasn't as if she was terribly social, so it was hard for her to make and keep friends. Sachin was the exception to the rule. He was outgoing enough for the both of them. He did tend to shy away from places that were too crowded, but she couldn't blame him there. Crowds bothered her as well.

He smiled and dimples formed on his cheeks. A cleft chin and eyes so silver they were like liquid mercury made for a striking man. It didn't hurt he had a body that could rival a bodybuilder's. The dark gray, V-neck shirt he wore gave her a glimpse of his tawny chest. It was hairless and smooth. She knew from seeing him work around the ranch without a shirt on. She also knew he had the start of black hair just below his navel and that she would give anything for the chance to lick her way down his body. On the verge of drooling, she averted her gaze.

Sachin came to a stop just before her and put his hand over hers, prying it loose from the pendant. "You rang, my lady?"

His playful, Knight-of-the-Round-Table banter always lightened her mood. It was easy to picture him with a sword in his hand, fighting some epic battle. A soft sigh slipped past her lips and she blushed.

Sachin bent, putting his face close to hers. "Is Sarah awaiting us?"

She stared up at him, fawning over him. When she realized, she stopped and tossed her shoulders back, hoping to salvage some piece of her dignity along the way. "She is. I think she gave up hope you'd make it in tonight."

He lifted his hand and touched her cheek. She closed her eyes and leaned into his palm. "I promised I would come. Did I not?"

Skimming her hand over his forearm, Paige nodded and stopped when her fingers brushed over shallow cuts. She grabbed his arm and turned it to get a better view. It looked as if he'd been clawed. "Sachin, what happened?"

"Nothing."

"Uh-huh, try another one, buddy. It looks like someone tried to take your arm off."

He stiffened. "Nonsense. It was…" he seemed to fumble for the right words, "a result of a night of passion. The woman I just left was rather rambunctious."

Woman?

Paige tossed his hand away from her face and backed away. "We should go in. Sarah has dinner waiting."

"Paige?" He took her hand in his. "You're angry. Why?"

"No reason. I'm fine."

———

AS PAIGE BRUSHED PAST HIM, Sachin cringed. Why had he said he'd been with a woman when he hadn't? He'd been caught detaining a traitor, one who'd tried to infiltrate the castle and kill the king. The man had nearly succeeded in removing Sachin's arm. Thankfully, Sachin was the more skilled of the two and killed the man before he could finish what he'd started.

He'd had to wait a few hours to ensure the wound was mostly healed over before flying to be with Paige. Telling her the truth wasn't an option, but the lie he'd chosen caused her pain. She cared for him a great deal. More than a woman should for a man she called a friend. He didn't mind. He cared for her as well. Much more than a warrior from another realm should for a human female.

Paige disappeared into the house and Sarah appeared on the front porch, her look pensive. "I told you not to build her up if your heart wasn't in it."

"Sarah, nothing can come of my feelings for Paige."

"Who says?" She posed a question he asked himself often as of late.

Prophecies telling of Kabril needing to take a mate seemed to be everywhere. The pressure for Kabril and other healthy young males of their race to figure out a solution to the lack-of-children issue was great. Sachin would never help bring a child to his people by bedding a human. No one had ever heard of a successful mating between a human and a member of his race. He ought to know. He'd asked around enough. His guards were beginning to whisper behind his back about his obsession with this realm.

Sarah crossed her arms over her chest. "You planning on standing out there all night or are you going to come in, be a man, and face the girl I know owns that rugged heart of yours?"

Letting out a long breath, Sachin chuckled. "You are a wise woman. My people would cherish one such as yourself."

Sarah winked. "Well, I'm lovable like that. Come on in, boy."

"Boy?" he echoed. "I'm older than you think."

She grinned. "I know. Now, get on in there and eat. And while you're at it, tell that young lady in there that you were just being a horse's ass. Beg her to forgive you."

He'd never begged for a thing in his

long life, but knew in that moment he would if it meant he'd be back in Paige's good graces. "Lead the way."

Sarah headed in and Sachin followed. The chill in the room had little to do with temperature and everything to do with Paige's mood. She cast him a look that froze his soul. He bowed his head and took a seat at the table. "This looks delicious, Sarah."

Paige stood quickly, causing her chair to make a scraping sound. "I, umm, forgot something."

"Paige?" Sarah called after her.

Sachin began spooning mashed potatoes, a food he'd found he very much enjoyed while in the human realm, onto his plate. Paige returned from the kitchen, carrying a plate. The devil was in her eyes and Sachin knew he wasn't going to like whatever she had planned. He also knew he deserved whatever it was.

"Here." A sugary sweet smile claimed her face. "I know how much you love roasted chicken. I saved you some."

His stomach twisted. While hawks

from Earth ate an array of foods they could catch, Sachin and his people did not eat birds of any kind. It was cannibalistic in their eyes. The smell of the chicken made his stomach protest. He turned his head away and clutched his thigh. "I'm… fine. I'm not that hungry."

Sarah took the plate from Paige, giving her a scolding look in the process. Paige blinked innocently. "Oh, that's right, you don't like chicken. Sorry. I forgot."

The smell of the chicken gradually cleared out of the dining room, leaving the scent of roast in its place. Paige returned to her seat, her gaze still icy. She pushed the food around on her plate before stabbing a cherry tomato so hard her fork clanked against the plate. The urge to cross his legs was great. Paige was most likely picturing her fork stabbing sensitive areas of him.

His gaze met hers and she nodded, as if reading his thoughts. His throat went dry. Taking hold of his water, he glanced down the table at Sarah, who looked amused by what was going on.

Sachin gulped his water. Wiping his mouth, he tried to come up with something profound to say that would make it all better. What came from his mouth wasn't what he had in mind. "I'm a horse's ass."

Paige set her fork down. "Go on."

She wanted more?

He'd just referred to himself as the ass end of a livestock and she wanted more? If Kabril could see him now, he would never hear the end of it.

"I lied."

"About?" Paige demanded.

"I was not with another woman." He could do this. He was head of the guards. A fierce warrior. So why was it he wanted to crawl, begging the auburn-haired beauty before him for forgiveness?

"Why would you being with another woman matter to me?" Paige picked her fork up again, holding it like a weapon.

Sarah rolled her eyes and snorted.

Paige ignored her.

Sachin cleared his throat and continued on. "I lied because I'm unsure how to handle how I feel for you." There. He'd said it.

"On that note, I'll let the two of you be," Sarah said. "I need to call Sheriff Bailey back anyways. He wants to come out in the morning and talk to us about those vandals we had here last week." She left the room, leaving Sachin to face Paige alone.

He hoped for leniency but knew his temperamental seductress would give him no such leeway. "And how do I make you feel, Sachin?"

"Like I can't breathe without you near," he confessed.

Paige was silent for what felt like forever, before standing and coming around to his side of the table. He reached out and eased the fork from her hand, unsure if she'd attempt to unman him with it.

She touched the scratches on his forearm. "How did you really get these?"

He wanted to tell her the truth but she wasn't ready yet. "Would you believe me if I said they were not from a woman and that I cannot tell you at this time exactly how I received them?"

He anticipated a battle.

"Yes," she whispered, bending and planting a kiss on his arm.

"Paige, I know it's customary for one to receive gifts on their birthday. I have something I…"

She pressed her fingers to his lips. "Shh. I want something you can't give me, Sachin. I want you."

His heart pounded madly, thumping so hard he feared it would leap from his chest. "You don't mean what I think you mean." He hoped she did.

A slow sweep of her lashes and curve of her lips made his cock jerk to life. She ran her fingers over his jaw and he nipped at them. He caught one and sucked on it gently, holding her gaze with his own.

Paige's lips puckered and she fell into his arms, her breath hissing out. Sachin dragged her to his chest, his heart still pounding and his cock aching for relief. "Paige."

"I can't breathe," she said, clinging to him.

"Neither can I." He did the only thing he could think to do. He kissed her. Her lips parted and her tongue greeted his. Sachin knew he was lost to her, that he would never feel something so intense for another.

Paige drew back, touching her swollen lower lip. "Sarah could walk in and find us."

He took her hands in his and kissed her neck. "Mmmhmm."

"Sachin," she scolded as she giggled. "Let's go for a walk."

"Or," he narrowed his eyes, "we could race to a secluded spot out behind that big oak tree and see who can undress the fastest."

Much to his surprise, Paige grinned. "Ready. Set. Go!"

Chapter Three

SACHIN SMILED DOWN AT THE BEAUTY
below him, still shocked to see her smooth,
pale skin exposed to him. Never did he
think Paige would surrender to his desires.
He'd hoped and prayed but thought it all
to be in vain. He'd known her for a little
over three cycles and had longed to touch
her, always holding back because of their
age difference. Now, she was a woman
according to her culture and able to make
her own decisions. Thankfully, they
included him, though Sachin could not
fathom why. He didn't deserve something
as precious as Paige. Her trust. Her love.

Love.

Such an interesting emotion. One he

had not understood until she came into his dull existence. Before her, he was content with village whores and quick tumbles with Earth females. Paige changed his perceptions of women. She made him feel something for the first time in a long time.

When he met her, she'd been broken, bruised and in shock. To this very day she held next to no memories of the night her mother had been murdered by her mother's live-in boyfriend. It was for the best. Had Paige recalled the night's events she would know just how close she came to death before Sachin swept down from the sky, killed the man who threatened her, and then cradled Paige to his chest as he flew high in the air, taking her to safety. He held his secrets of being part man, part bird from her and didn't relish the idea of telling her the truth. He knew she suffered from night terrors, but he couldn't reveal the fact—that he wasn't human.

She bit at her lower lip. He spent many a day dreaming of how soft her lips were, the bottom one fuller than the top, and how easily they molded to meet his. Too often he had to leave her when he wasn't ready. The wars ravaging his realm had increased to the point it was harder than ever to slip away undetected for even a few hours, let alone days. The enemy seemed to be camped outside their gates, waiting for the right time to strike. They'd become organized. Where before they were small pockets of resistance, they were fast becoming an army to contend with.

A true threat.

Even with the knowledge of the state of affairs in his home realm, Sachin couldn't seem to stay away from Paige. Her soft laugh and tender looks haunted him sweetly, even from a distance.

Will I ever be ready to leave her?

The answer was simple. No. He would never be ready to say goodbye to Paige, but the choice wasn't his to make. Humans weren't part of his world. They were looked down upon, thought of as nothing more than vile creatures who lacked the ability to shape-shift into a bird of prey. Though they did have much in the way of technologies, they used them in the wrong manner—self-destruction on their part was imminent.

Their realm was polluted, riddled with disease and overpopulated. Still, even with all the negatives, Sachin couldn't stop traveling through the portals that brought him to Paige. When he'd first seen her in the woods, her auburn hair reflecting the moonlight and her big brown eyes wide as she tried to huddle against a tree for protection, he'd lost a piece of himself to her. Things had ended well for Paige. Sarah had welcomed her into her home and the two bonded instantly.

Sarah was middle-aged, with no children of her own and a horse ranch in need of some tender love and care. Paige fit well with Sarah, becoming a surrogate child for her. In the process they had become an odd sort of family with Sachin as well. He couldn't stay away. The need to check on Paige was almost all consuming.

He'd been coming to Paige's ranch for months now, stealing visits and kisses from her, never once conveying the extent of his feelings or what he truly was—a *Buteos*

Regalis—a man with the ability to shift into a hawk. He wasn't human. Didn't even hail from her realm, yet she had become the flame and he the moth. Duty called and he had no choice but to part ways, forcing him to savor every moment with her.

"Sachin," she whispered beneath him, arching her back, exposing her neck to him. He showered it with kisses as he ground his hips against hers, his cock hard and pressed to her abdomen. Their clothes and boots lay discarded haphazardly on the grass surrounding them. When Paige had whispered "yes" to wanting to lie with him, Sachin had been left fighting the urge to partially shift forms—something legends spoke of happening when one merged with their life mate.

She is human. She cannot possibly be my life mate.

Kissing her earlobe, Sachin inhaled, committing the scent of her arousal to memory. She was young, only twenty-one cycles old. Far too young for his nearly four hundred cycles.

His morning prayer sessions were no longer spent asking the bird gods for guidance, they were now spent begging them to break the pull the human below him had over him.

He bent, capturing one of her tiny pink nipples between his teeth. He tugged gently and she melted under his touch. His eyes slipped shut as he licked her pebble-like peak. His cock jerked, threatening to come before he wanted to.

She was innocent to the ways of a man and Sachin knew he had to prepare her to receive him. Paige writhed under him as he continued his sensual assault on her nipple. He licked, positive she tasted of berries. Her skin was cool to the touch and yet his palms felt as if they were ablaze. He would surely burn alive before he even entered her. He'd never heard of a fellow shifter spontaneously combusting during sex, but there was a first time for everything. He'd also never thought he'd be so taken with a human female that he'd risk his position among his people just to be near her.

Sachin rolled her nipple in his mouth and smiled. She groaned, fisting her hands into his shoulder-length hair and tugging firmly. The excitement of the act raced straight to his groin. He wanted to burrow into her tender flesh but hesitated, unwilling to risk harming her.

"Sachin, please."

"Mmm, *ta'konima*," he said, his voice low as he moved to her other breast, giving it equal attention.

"I can't take anymore. Please."

He kissed his way down her flat belly to the swell of her abdomen. Another dusting of freckles lay there and he licked each and every one. It looked as if someone sprinkled cinnamon on her pale skin. "You can and you will."

Her brown eyes widened as he forced her legs open wide. Red curls adorned her mound, thick and slick with cream. Already she was wet for him and he had yet to touch her sex.

So moist.

The sound of the horses in the stables nearby reminded Sachin they were exposed to anyone who might wander past. He didn't think Sarah would happen upon them, and if she did, Sachin suspected the woman would simply smile and walk away. She seemed to push Sachin to accept his feelings for Paige even when he refused to believe he had any.

I am weak. He caressed her. *And she is my weakness.*

So beautiful, so angelic and blissfully unaware of what truly touched her. More than a man. A monster in the eyes of her people.

Sachin took in a deep breath and almost lost control of himself. Never had he smelled anything more seductive than the scent of her arousal. Paige squirmed, pushing her sex towards his face. He laughed and buried his mouth into her slit. He had found heaven. Her rosy clit glistened, covered in her creamy wetness. A low moan of approval escaped him. Paige cried out, jerking under his touch as he alternated licks and sucks on her swollen bud.

Her fingernails dug into his shoulders

briefly before her thighs clamped to the sides of his head. Sachin felt whole, as if he'd finally found a piece of himself he'd not known was missing.

Inserting the tip of a finger into her tight sheath, he stared up, never seeing anything as erotic as Paige looking down at him. Her eyes held lust and her mouth was pert—thoroughly kissed. If he dared to push farther, he'd break her virginal barrier and claim her for his own for all time. He eased a second finger into her, this time meeting resistance.

She is human. She cannot be claimed.

The thoughts niggled at the back of his mind, but the way her pussy closed around his fingers drew his thoughts to Paige. He had to be in her. He pushed his finger through the resistance and she stilled. Sensing her pain, Sachin dipped his head, licking her and inserting his tongue in place of his fingers. Paige moved her hips, slightly at first before increasing the pace. He rubbed her clit as he licked her. She tightened around his tongue and pulsed, her orgasm taking hold of her.

Cream coated his tongue and a pinching at the base of his spine warned he was near a partial shift. Sachin tried to calm himself, but the sight of her quivering pussy, all wet from his labor, was too much. He moved upwards, his wings uncurling from between his shoulder blades, and he used his body to cover hers, hoping she wouldn't notice. She closed her eyes as her orgasm continued to move over her.

He lined the head of his cock with her entrance and thrust in, no longer able to wait. Paige cried out, grasping his upper arms, her eyes still closed tight and his name on her lips.

"Paige Rapp, do you accept me—all of me from now until the end of time?"

Writhing under him, she nodded, her eyes still shut.

He needed to hear her say it. Something deep and primitive within him demanded she recognize his words. They were words that had spilled free from him, words through the fog that was now his mind, he understood were important.

Very important. Though, his mind was a jumbled mess.

She moaned.

"Do you…accept me…" it was hard to talk when all he wanted to do was take pleasure from her, "…all of me from now until the end of time?"

"Yes, Sachin. Yes!"

He pumped vigorously. She had been made to fit him, of that he was sure. Fearful Paige would open her eyes and see him for what he truly was, Sachin planted kisses on her eyelids as he continued to move in and out of her. He lost hold of what little control he had and rooted himself deep within her, coming in waves. Each time seed sprung forth from his body and into hers, he felt as if he were sharing his soul with her. Sachin's magik rose up around them. Additional feathers formed on his lower back, signaling he was on the verge of a full shift. Static energy surrounded them but Sachin was unsure why. Something niggled at the back of his mind. Something important. He couldn't focus. All he knew was that it felt as if strings were wrapping from his heart to hers—binding them.

Paige put her legs around his waist, panting and holding tight to him. The second her foot bumped one of his long, feathered wings, Sachin knew he had to end the moment. He pulled out, still dripping seed, the proof of her innocence smeared on his shaft. He took flight, leaving his clothing and Paige behind. He waited until he was far from her to look back with his preternatural eyesight. Paige was sitting up, staring around, looking confused and hurt. As much as Sachin wanted to fly back and comfort her, he could not. Humans weren't to know of his kind. He'd been wrong for finding pleasure in her and this was his punishment.

Chapter Four

ACCIPITRIDAE   *REALM*   —   *ONE Year Later...*

Sachin spun, bringing his sword up and meeting his opponent head-on. The clank of metal meeting metal vibrated through him but he held strong. Centuries of battles and training left him conditioned for almost anything. His skills and his body were honed, as with any warrior worth his weight in gold. His senses spiked and the smells of battle moved over him. His opponent held fear.

As it should be.

He twisted once more, meeting another attack and thrusting away danger. It was almost too easy. Where was the challenge in it all? Deep, steady breaths were all Sachin drew in. His opponent's breaths were choppy, shallow and as ill-timed as the man's swings. Fatigue was the main cause. This man should have posed a greater threat than he did. In Sachin's current state of mind, nothing was as dangerous as he was.

Crossing his feet, Sachin's opponent committed a cardinal sin in fighting. It would have been too easy to toss the man off balance and put a finish to it all. The burning not only in his muscles but deep in his chest refused to allow Sachin to end the session so soon. His mind was still reeling with the need to focus on anything other than what currently robbed him of sleep. He should have been sluggish, dead on his feet. He was anything but. He'd become a caged beast, in search of diversions allowing him to unleash his rage. They were fewer than he wished so he took to creating them.

His opponent, a guard under his command, dropped his sword and slumped his shoulders, looking defeated.

"My lord, your mood is foul and your strength great. I wish not to test my life by training further with you on this morn."

The guard's honesty was refreshing but not what Sachin wanted to hear. Normally it was he who was the bearer of sobering news. Since his mood had indeed soured over the last several moons, he was not sought after for his wise words. If anything, his best friend and king of *Accipitridae*, Kabril, often jested that seeking guidance from an injured boar would prove more appealing than he. Sachin could hardly argue the point for he would rather be in the company of a boar as well, instead of himself.

Sachin's sleep had been fitful at best as of late and the overwhelming need to leave the *Accipitridae* Realm all but consumed him. His brotherly love for Kabril and Kabril's mate, Rayna, kept him from doing what he normally did when the need to visit Earth struck—take off without question, heading to a realm he should not enjoy as much as he did. His place was alongside his king, not frolicking about in a realm full of people who lacked wings. Full of humans. Full of her.

He shook his head, desperate to keep his thoughts free of her. He had important matters to attend to here. There was no room for anything beyond his sworn duties to his king and queen. No space for somber reflections of past deeds he could not change.

Rayna's belly was swollen with Kabril's child and she'd taken sick on more than one occasion. She and the babe were fine, according to doctors, but the news did nothing to lessen the need to stay on, assure the couple remained safe in the face of war. Their child marked the dawning of a new day for his people. For too long they'd been without the laughter of children or the pitter-patter of tiny feet scurrying about the halls of the castle. Centuries had gone by with no unions producing offspring. The longevity of their race of bird shifters meant they were, for lack of a better word, immortal, but even with that trait, wars throughout the realm had dwindled their numbers. The coming child was a sign from the Epopisdeus that hope lived. The bird gods were feared and worshiped by his people. This show of faith on their behalf was what was needed to lift spirits.

I shall ensure their gift is protected.

The *Falco Peregrinus* were the *Buteos Regalis's* sworn enemies. Talk of a Falco attack had been circulating for some time. They had tried and almost succeeded in killing Rayna once before. Had one of the Falco's own not defected, refusing to see harm come to Rayna, she would have died. Now wasn't a time to waver in his duties. Sachin had to be vigilant.

"My lord?" the guard asked, looking hopeful Sachin would end training early for the day.

Taking pity on the man, Sachin nodded. "We are done here. Good fight."

"Good fight." The guard bowed, touching Sachin's shoulders and lowering his gaze, as was the custom between warrior allies, and then scurried off in the other direction.

Sachin turned to walk away and found

Rayna standing in the entrance to the castle. Her hand rested on her swollen belly and her blue eyes held mischief. She smiled, her long hair blowing in the slight breeze. A rosy glow overtook her. "Beating up on everyone already and it's not even breakfast time." She grinned. "Remind me not to bother you until lunch."

"My lady." He inclined his head and attempted to go past her.

Rayna caught his arm and halted his movement. He could break her hold with virtually no effort, but respected her too much to dare. "Sachin, don't *my lady* me. I'm Rayna to you and you know it."

An exasperated breath fell free from his lips. "Very well, Rayna."

She gave him a cross look. "Are you planning to continue scaring your guards to the point they don't want to be near you or are you going to tell me what's eating at you?"

Glancing around to assure himself they were alone, Sachin sighed and ran a hand over the back of his neck. Several kinks had settled there a couple of moons prior, and at the rate Sachin was going, they would become permanent. "There is naught amiss, my...erm...Rayna." She was from Earth, and while she now dressed the part of queen, she refused to be bound by titles. She also continued to think of them as close friends rather than that of a head guard and his queen. Kabril seemed to encourage the behavior. It was pure madness around the castle anymore.

Sachin had always assumed when Kabril finally took a mate he would keep her far from him—especially considering Sachin's lust for Earth women. Kabril did the opposite. He encouraged Rayna to seek Sachin out. All had remained platonic.

Rayna kept her hand on him. "Sachin, Kabril's worried about you. So am I."

"I am fine." It was an untruth, but one he was willing to stand by.

She pursed her lips. "I never took you for a liar, Sachin. I guess I'll have to throw my weight around, huh?"

Confused, he simply stared at her. Even though he spent a good deal of time in the human realm, he found there were some sayings Rayna used that he was unaware of their actual meaning. Throwing her weight was one of them. She had indeed increased in size since her arrival, but that was due to the fact she was heavy with child. Did she think she could throw herself at him and perhaps sit on him until he conceded his days had grown dark and his mood sour? Even she was not large enough to pose any threat to him.

"Sachin, you are to take one week's leave, effective immediately." Her eyes twinkled as she continued to rub her distended belly. "And you *must* take the time off on Earth."

He baulked. "Rayna, you cannot think I would leave you and Kabril undefended when——"

She motioned to the hundreds upon hundreds of guards heading back to their homes. "They don't count? And I've seen my husband fight. He's a force to be reckoned with when he's pissed. So, unless you want to ignore *your queen's* orders, you should really get going." Rayna spun on her heels and left him to stare dumbfounded in her wake.

A hearty laugh drew his attention and he found Kabril walking towards him. Kabril's golden gaze locked firmly on Sachin. "From the look on your face, my wife not only found you but she did as she threatened to do—order you to take leave."

"Kabril, she cannot force me to—"

Putting his hand up, Kabril silenced him. "Ah, but she can and she did. After all, she is queen. Is she not?"

Sachin exhaled deeply. "Yes."

"Go, Sachin. Take the time you need on Earth to do whatever it is you do that helps you find peace. We will be here when you return."

Chapter Five

DEFEATED, SACHIN HELD HIS TONGUE AND stormed towards his chamber. Sconces lit the narrow hall. He had chosen to take the back way to his room, the servants' corridor, in hope of avoiding any of his men. His foul temperament would only leave him challenging them to another round of sparring. He was up for it, though he doubted if they were.

Soft moans and murmurs caught Sachin's attention. He paused just outside of the buttery. He peeked around the slightly ajar door and watched a serving wench pulling her skirts high as Lazar, a defector from the *Falco Peregrinus*, undid his breeches. Sachin was taken aback to see

Lazar with the woman for she was below the salt in every way possible. A lowbred whore. This show was fine so long as the person you chose to be with wasn't of a lower standing.

Sachin watched as Lazar cupped the back of the wench's neck, whispering sweet nothings to her as he readied her for the taking. His own cock grew hard at the sight and he made no qualms about fisting himself through his trews.

Sachin held little worry about being stumbled upon. His race, the *Buteos Regalis*, were not only fierce warriors, but well known for their prowess. Public displays of affection were not frowned upon but rather they were encouraged.

The wench tossed her head back, sending long waves of golden tresses in every direction. She cried out and writhed beneath Lazar's nimble fingers. Sachin had tumbled with the wench several times, many years ago, before she began accepting coin for her services—before he met Paige. And while the wench wasn't lacking in the wants of a man, she did little to sate his need. Still, anything was better than nothing.

He rubbed his clothed cock, enjoying the part of voyeur more than he should. Each time the wench attempted to kiss Lazar on the mouth, the man turned his head away. Sachin understood why. It was a means to avoid intimacy. Something he himself was prone to doing. There had been only one woman he'd kissed passionately while sinking deep into her, and there would never be another. He would use other women for his baser needs but keep his heart out of the mix.

Rubbing the flesh standing in stark relief in his trews, Sachin watched as Lazar brought the whore to peak with nothing more than his fingers. The woman bucked against Lazar's hand and begged for more. Nodding, Lazar lifted her and repositioned her so she was facing away from him. Lazar's gaze met Sachin's over the whore's head. A tiny smile tugged at the man's lips and he yanked the wench's skirts higher before slapping her ass cheek. The resounding thud echoed through the area, exciting Sachin. He unlaced his trews and took hold of himself.

Lazar spanked the whore again and rubbed the area. "You have been naughty, tempting a man so," Lazar said, repeating his actions. "You should be punished."

The whore wiggled, her ass cheeks reddened. "Oh, yes. Punish me. Punish me!"

Lazar dipped his fingers into the whore's quim and used her juices to coat his cock. He lifted a brow in question in Sachin's direction and motioned to the whore's ass. Sachin knew it was a silent invite to join in the fun. He considered it but stood his ground, deciding instead to spit on his palm, adding his own form of lubrication as he fondled his shaft.

Lazar delivered another set of soft blows to the woman's backside and she squealed with delight, pressing herself back towards him. Lazar whispered, "Patience."

Sachin's balls began to tighten and he knew he was on the verge of coming. He imagined it was he who was sliding into a wet sheath instead of Lazar and his wench. Sachin pictured red hair and skin dusted with freckles. He could almost feel Paige wrapped around his cock, her body tight yet accepting. He continued to stroke himself as the sounds of sex surrounded him.

Lazar pounded his body into the serving wench's relentlessly. Sachin wasn't sure how the woman could take such roughness, but she seemed to relish it, screaming out for more.

Lazar smiled. It was unkind, and a flash of hate moved through his eyes as he fucked the woman. For Sachin it was like looking in a mirror. He too wore that look when he needed to see to his manly needs. Only with Paige it had been different. After her, he hated himself for being weak and needing to find release in someone else. And since Paige it was hard for him to find even that. So hard that he often lied to the other guards about his conquests as his manly parts seemed to lack the desire to bed women.

Not women, he reminded himself. *Your cock wants Paige, as do you.*

Lazar stopped taking the wench from behind and spun her around to face him. He held her chin as she spat at him, talking about how he was nothing more than a dirty falcon that no women of hawk descent wanted to touch. She looked excited by the words, as if the knowledge somehow gave her power over him. She tossed her legs over Lazar's shoulders, allowing the man to go deeper with his thrusts.

Sachin stroked himself, feeling the man's hate of the woman he was with but understanding the need to feel like a man regardless the price.

"Fuck me harder, you dirty beast," the wench said, biting at Lazar's hand.

Lazar slapped her face lightly and narrowed his gaze on her. "Bite me and I will deny you the chance to come again, wench."

"No," she cried, reaching between their bodies in an attempt to grasp Lazar's cock. Lazar thrust her hand away and pummeled her body with his own. Sachin matched his strokes, fisting himself, nearing release.

Lazar ripped the wench's bodice open, causing her large breasts to spill out. They were not the prettiest breasts he'd ever seen but they did help to push Sachin nearer to peak. He watched as her nipples hardened in the cool air. Biting at his lower lip, Sachin pictured Paige in his mind. It was her face he saw in place of the whore's, her body, and in his thoughts it was he who was giving her pleasure. He moaned as his balls drew up tight and his cock twitched. He came, jetting his seed onto the floor.

Pulling free of the wench, Lazar came too, allowing his seed to splash over the whore's thighs. She hissed at him and tried to strike him. "I didn't come again. I—"

Lazar stared down at her before shifting his haunted gaze towards Sachin. "Your turn."

Sachin shook his head. "I am done and have no need for the likes of her."

A genuine smile came over Lazar. "As

am I. Off with you." He yanked her skirts down and swatted her backside.

She huffed and shrieked away, her gaze coming to Sachin. "M-my lord, I-I did not—"

Sachin waved his hand dismissively. "Be gone."

She nodded before rushing off in the other direction, muttering curses under her breath.

Lazar tucked his cock back into his trews and Sachin did the same. Sachin looked at the floor and the side of the table and laughed. "The cook will have our heads for messing up her kitchen."

"Then we best be off." Lazar pulled two gold coins from the leather purse on his belt and tossed them onto the table. "For her time."

Sachin shook his head. "She was only worth one."

"I know," Lazar said, heading out of the room. He stopped just outside of the kitchen. "Do you think there are any women left in the world worth more?"

Sachin thought of Paige. He smiled

and let out a long breath. "I am positive there are women worth more than we could ever hope to give them."

Lazar stared silently at him before speaking. "Mayhap you should find and hold tight to one should you ever cross her path. I know I would."

"Such insight from one so…"

Grinning, Lazar adjusted his covered cock. "Hungry for a commitment-free fuck?"

"Your words."

Lazar watched him closely. "Rumors of you bedding Earth women and going through lines of them to get your fill are high with the guards. Are they true?"

At one point in his life the rumors had been true. After Paige, no human woman could come close to what she made him feel. "You cannot believe everything you hear."

"Really?"

It was obvious Sachin wasn't successful in his lies. He exhaled and scratched at his inner arm. "I have been ordered to take leave…on Earth. Care to join me?"

"Ordered?" Lazar pressed, merriment twinkling in the man's eyes. "By whom?"

"The queen."

Lazar snorted. "By all means, I would not wish to miss this, but alas, Kabril has asked me to prep him for a possible peace negotiation with the Falcos."

"Peace?"

Lazar looked as though he thought the chances of obtaining peace were as slim as Sachin believed them to be. "Yes."

"Best of luck. They aren't to be trusted, but I suppose you know that." Sachin pivoted and made his way through the kitchen in a rush to simply make it to his chambers. He walked into low-hanging herbs put there to dry and cursed silently as he backed into another table. One of the kitchen cooks appeared and gave him a cross look before waving a wooden spoon at him. He flashed an innocent smile in the older woman's direction and she shook her head.

"I've known you since you were but a babe, Sachin." She shook her spoon at him. "You were still on your mother's tit.

You are nothing if not a troublemaker. I can guess the smell of sex in the air is from you and one of the castle whores."

"No. Not I." He blushed from his toes to his ears and glanced back to find Lazar was long gone. The last thing he wanted was someone mentioning him being on his mother's tit in front of his men. "I am innocent, *sweet maiden*."

"I'll sweet maiden you." She threw the spoon at him and he laughed, stumbling on his way out of the kitchen. For such a fearsome warrior, he seemed to be having trouble staying on his feet.

Rayna was right. He needed to take leave and get away from it all, but the knowledge didn't make going any easier. He'd spent nearly four hundred cycles protecting Kabril. To leave him at his most vulnerable time seemed wrong. Still, a direct order, by his queen, had been issued. Sachin had no choice but to accept.

He kicked the heavy wooden door of his chamber open so hard and so fast, it splintered down the center before slamming into a tiny side table. An open saucer filled with oil and a floating wick crashed to the floor, its contents coating the broken door and table. Kabril would remind him of his temper when he saw the damage. Not that Kabril hadn't been known to break a door or two in his four hundred cycles.

Sachin wiped the sweat from his brow and fixed his gaze on the side table. There, a piece of leather was threaded through a lone amber crystal. It shimmered as the light from the window shone in, causing various patterns to appear on his chamber-room walls. There was a time Sachin was never found without the leather tied around his neck. Guilt had caused him to finally remove the item that reminded him of Paige. He had given her a matching one in the beginning of their friendship and she'd done something similar with hers, threading a black cord through it. The crystals were magikally charged, allowing the wearer's thoughts to be amplified. When Sachin was still wearing his, he would sense Paige's need to see him and he would go to her. She'd stopped wanting him near after he'd left her a year ago in the grass, alone and vulnerable.

I wonder if she still wears hers.

Closing his eyes, he tried and failed to push thoughts of Paige from his head. He'd made himself a promise to stay away from her. She was an addiction, one he couldn't seem to shake. As Rayna's order to go to Earth filtered through Sachin's mind, the need to go to *her* was great.

A warrior he may be, but he'd tasted defeat the day he'd lost his heart to Paige. Looking in on her couldn't harm anything. He just needed to be sure she was well.

Chapter Six

EARTH

Paige double-checked the horse's bandage and rubbed his upper leg. The injury had been slight and the horse was expected to make a full recovery. It, like many of the people who passed through the ranch, had come to her broken, abused. "You're a good boy, huh? That's right. A good boy."

The horse turned its head towards her and seemed to understand her concern. It had survived neglect from its previous owner and had been brought to her barely able to support its own weight. That had been a little over a year ago. With much love and care, it was well on its way to being whole again. It did have a tendency to be rambunctious and had ended up hurting itself in the process. They went out of their way to safeguard the ranch, in hopes it would prevent injuries to the horses, but domesticated horses were notoriously accident-prone. This one was no exception. He was young and finally free of abuse. She couldn't blame him for wanting to enjoy his time to the fullest.

The early summer air was drier than normal and she wondered if another drought would hit the area. The ranch had made it through the year prior, when just about everything in the surrounding area had dried up. Their income came mostly from boarding animals and the onsite animal hospital. Sarah was a veterinarian. Paige was in her second year of school to be a veterinary assistant.

Smiling, she stood and patted the horse's back. "Go ahead. Let's see how it's holding up."

The horse walked away and she kept a

close eye on the wrapped leg. Even though Paige knew the horse would be fine, she couldn't help but worry. His mood had been surly of late and his temperament unpredictable, reminding her of somebody she once knew.

"Firecracker looks to be doing well," a deep, familiar voice came from behind her.

Think of the devil and he shall appear.

Turning, Paige found a six-foot–five-inch wall of toned muscle sitting on the top rail of the wooden fence. He hadn't been there a moment ago. The man's black goatee matched his shoulder-length hair and his thick eyelashes, drawing attention to his silver eyes. It wasn't a color one found naturally, and there was a time Paige wouldn't have questioned him on the fact. That time had long since passed. Even with all the questions she had for the man before her, there was still no denying the fact he took her breath away. She'd heard it said before—looking that good should be outlawed. She tended to agree. She'd also thought she'd never see him again. His return wasn't exactly welcomed. It confused her.

"Sachin?"

He smiled. "Paige, it's been far too long."

His body was a model of perfection. He ran his hands over his jean-clad thighs and tipped his head, offering a sheepish smile. It was a smile that used to make her melt, but his appearing and disappearing act had long since worn on her. The last time had been the final straw. He'd had the nerve to run out on her the minute he'd finished having sex with her. She'd even gone so far as to hunt for him, but it was as if he never existed. There had been no paper trail, no record of any kind of him.

"What the hell are you doing here?"

The smile slid from his face. "Ah, I see you are upset with me."

"And why shouldn't I be?"

He had no response. Not that she really expected him to be able to make a legitimate case. He did what so many men did, he ran after he'd gotten what he'd wanted.

Was he back in hopes of more?

Paige glanced away, needing a moment to soak in the knowledge he was indeed before her in the flesh. There were many things she'd wanted to say to him for so long. So many things she should tell him, but none of them fell from her lips. A silent curse was all she could muster before collecting her thoughts once more. She set her sights on the horse. "This isn't the same Firecracker you remember. He passed away."

"Really?" Sachin asked, as his gaze swept over the horse. "He looks almost identical."

"I know." A half smile tugged at her lips and she fought it. "It's why I named him Firecracker Redux. He's a pistol who survived horrible abuse. You should have seen the conditions they had him living in, Sachin. Rusted, barbed-wire fencing, a metal shelter with a broken door and his food was moldy and infested with worms. Don't even get me started on the physical abuse."

Why was she talking to him so calmly

when all she really wanted to do was kick, scream, throw a fit at how he'd abandoned her, and the secrets he'd obviously kept from her. She'd practiced what she'd say or do if she were to ever come face-to-face with Sachin again. All of it went out the window the moment she stared into his silver gaze. Something deep inside her chest tugged, feeling as if invisible strings connected them.

"Like his predecessor," Sachin offered, his voice thick.

She nodded, her heart in her throat and an array of emotions washing over her. She tried to convince herself it was because of his concern for an animal she'd loved, but she knew that was only part of the reason she was close to crying. He was back, and deep down Paige knew that was all she'd ever really wanted. But she couldn't take him toying with her feelings again. There was no way she could let him beneath the shield she'd built, the one that had finally allowed her to stop crying herself to sleep at night—the one that would let her start to live again.

"Then it's a fitting name for a fine horse," he offered evenly.

Firecracker nudged her, urging her to move towards Sachin. The first Firecracker, an equally black stallion with a similar wild streak, had always seemed to take to the mysterious rogue, no matter how many times Sachin vanished for months on end, chipping away at her hardened heart in the process. Its namesake seemed just as enamored with Sachin.

Sachin hopped down from the fence and dusted off his backside. Oh God, how she wanted to be the one touching him, but it wasn't to be. Paige had once thought Sachin might have feelings for her that extended beyond a roll in the hay. He couldn't care about her and vanish like he did.

"Paige." He put his hand out and stroked the top of Firecracker's head. "Are you going to talk to me or are you planning on giving me menacing stares the entire time I'm here?"

"And how long is it that you're here for, Sachin? I'd like to know since I'm planning on the latter of the two." Annoyed with her behavior, Paige took hold of Firecracker's reins and tried to lead him from the exercise area. Sachin blocked her path and the horse seemed bound and determined to stand his ground as well.

Men. They were all traitors and co-conspirators.

Sachin laughed, as if he'd read her thoughts.

"How long do you want me here?" His silver gaze slid over her slowly, heating her body along the way.

Paige swallowed down the lump in her throat, fighting to maintain control. For some reason, whenever Sachin was near, she responded to his very presence. No other man had made her react so and she seriously doubted any ever would. It made it damn hard to get over Sachin's disappearing acts, his secrets, and, in the end, his use of her and move forward, but she was determined to do just that. Her heart wasn't a toy and he'd played with it enough. Besides, it was no longer just her that she had to worry about—she'd moved on and another man's happiness was now intertwined with hers. She had questions for Sachin, but they would have to wait until she could prepare herself to deal with him.

"You should go," she heard herself say, unsure where the courage to form the words came from.

He ignored her.

"Sachin."

Leaning down, he put his lips dangerously close to hers. Kissing him would be so easy. He'd branded her with the taste of his kisses long ago, imprinting them on her. Her lips tingled with remembered pleasures. To give in to him would be so easy. A sweet surrender.

He inched his fingers up her sides, partially under her shirt and Paige did the same to him, needing skin-to-skin contact. Her body was starved for him and, if she were forced to admit it, so was she. Each press of his fingers into her flesh caused another torrent of cream to form between her legs. Needing someone this bad wasn't normal. She should be furious at him for his betrayal and for so many other reasons, but her mind was awash with nothing but feelings of the moment.

"Paige!"

Chapter Seven

SACHIN STIFFENED AT THE SOUND OF THE male voice. Last he knew Paige and Sarah lived alone on the ranch, rehabilitating horses. They'd stopped taking in troubled teens several years back. The only hired hand they'd had was a young boy, around the age of fifteen or sixteen. Surely not old enough to have a voice as deep as the one he'd just heard. He waited for any sign from Paige as to who the man was, but got his answer soon enough.

A tall man appeared from around the side of the barn, carrying a basket with him. He wore a cowboy hat and looked to fit the part perfectly—a country boy—a human country boy. Something Sachin could never be. He would forever be a warrior from another realm.

He'd thought she was a passing thing, a phase he needed to go through on his path of life. How wrong he'd been. She was so much more. An obsession. A gift the gods would not grant him. Something tugged at him from within. A truth he seemed unable to see. As he thought back to the night they'd shared, the words he'd spoken became crystal clear to him.

He sucked in a large breath.

He'd claimed a human.

He'd claimed Paige.

He had a wife.

A wife who didn't think too highly of him.

A wife who currently had another male coming for her.

The man with the basket approached slowly, his eyes full of questions but his facial expression agreeable. There was something familiar about the man but Sachin couldn't place him. "Who do we have here?"

Paige pushed her long auburn hair behind her ear and shuffled her feet, a sure sign she was nervous. "Umm, Bailey, this is an old friend of mine, Sachin."

Bailey? He knew that name from somewhere. At some point Paige had mentioned it to him. As if reading his mind, Paige glanced towards him. "Bailey is the sheriff here. He helped me when I had those problems with vandals last year."

I bet he did.

Sachin barely kept hold of his temper as he watched Bailey bend and plant a kiss on the corner of Paige's mouth. The man dared to kiss his wife? "Mmm, baby, I didn't know you had company today or I wouldn't have—"

Baby?

Sachin entertained killing him on the spot. The man had some nerve.

"He just stopped by and is leaving." She gave Sachin a daring look.

"Nonsense, I brought enough food for an army. You know how my momma is. She heard I wanted to bring lunch out to you and she insisted on coming over to my house to prepare it." Bailey laughed and the sound grated on Sachin's nerves. "She kept mumbling something about how bad my cooking is." Bailey glanced at Sachin. "Care to join us for lunch?"

He'd much rather rip the man's head from his shoulders but Sachin kept that bit to himself and nodded. "Thank you," he managed. "I'd be honored."

Paige gawked at him, her mouth open wide. "What?"

Sachin grinned. If his woman thought he was leaving her with another man, she was wrong. "The man made me an offer I could not refuse." He put his hand out. "Here, I can take that basket to the house."

"No," Paige said quickly. She took a moment, adjusting her shirt and rubbing her palms on her thighs before locking gazes with him. "I'll get it, Sachin. Really. Sarah's resting and I don't want to wake her."

Interrogating prisoners was one of

Sachin's specialties. He had a sixth sense for a lie. His skills were not needed to know Paige wished desperately to push him away. Did she not understand who she was to him?

You only just figured it out, he reminded himself.

He knew Paige had led a hard life, one that left her first being fostered by the woman who owned the ranch and then eventually adopted by her. Trust was something she didn't offer freely, and a part of him knew she might not be willing to accept him back into her life. No amount of foresight helped to ease the pain of seeing her in another man's arms. But he deserved it. Deserved seeing she'd managed to move on.

Bailey gave her a little swat on the backside and Sachin was reminded of seeing Lazar with the whore. His thoughts shifted and images of Paige surrendering herself to Bailey plagued him. Hot rage tore through him and he made a move to go at Bailey.

Oh God, Sachin's going to kill him. Just keep him away from Bailey, then everything should be fine.

Hearing Paige's thoughts in his head made Sachin stop dead in his tracks. He stared at her long and hard, sure it had been a play of the mind. A trick of some sort. Tipping his head, he waited to hear more but none came.

Paige handed the basket to Bailey. "Will you take this up? I'll be there in just a second. I want to get Firecracker Redux back to the stables. Sachin can help me."

Bailey cast a worried glance in Sachin's direction before reluctantly taking the basket from Paige's outstretched hand. "Sure thing." He bent and kissed her again.

Sachin fought the urge to kill the man and remained motionless. It was one of the hardest things he'd ever done—outside of fly away from his mate a year ago. Once Bailey was far from view, Paige turned to Sachin, her expression anything but kind. "You lay one hand on him and I will skin you alive. Understand?"

He bit back a laugh. He'd been privy to many instances of skinning alive and knew Paige lacked the knowledge or the stomach for the act, but her threat was admirable. "Yes. I understand."

"Good." She walked towards the horse. "Now, help me lead him back to the stables."

He fell into step next to her. They made their way into the back stables and he assisted in corralling the horse. When he looked, he found Paige sliding the barn door shut and then focusing on him.

"Why did you leave?" she asked, her voice barely above a whisper.

Because I had to.

"I did not come here to cause you pain, Paige."

She lifted her chin. "Then why did you come? Why now after all of these months?"

Because I missed you.

"If you truly wish for me to leave," he sighed, "I will."

He thought for a minute she would say yes. She didn't. Putting her hand to her mouth, she stifled a tiny cry as her shoulders slumped. It broke his heart to see her weep, and before he knew it, he had Paige held tight to him, her face buried against his chest. It felt good to hold her again. Too long had gone by without the feel of her.

Each sob cracked the hardness surrounding his heart. He hated knowing he'd done this to her. He'd upset her. Planting a tiny kiss upon her head, he tried to will her to be happy again, to forgive him.

Paige pushed on his chest and shook her head, wiping her tear-stained cheeks. "No. I will not cry over you again. I'm done with that. I'm done with—" her gaze met his "—you. I have questions for you about what happened the night we met. But not now. Not when Bailey is around."

"I could remove him from the equation," Sachin offered.

She stared up at him. "I agreed to marry him. He's part of my life now, Sachin."

A harder blow an enemy had never

delivered. He tried to draw air in but found he couldn't. He staggered backwards, bumping into a wooden support beam. "You're to be married?"

"Yes."

How could she move on without me? How could she give herself to another man? She is my wife! He paused. *She is unaware of this truth because you, yourself had refused to admit it.*

Paige cleared her throat and forced her shoulders back, looking proud. "It wasn't easy, Sachin. It took me months to give up on you...on us. I have a life started now and it's a good one. I won't let you waltz in, cause turmoil and then vanish."

He blinked. She'd answered his unspoken questions. But how? Legends of old spoke of the ability for mated pairs of his race to be able to communicate with nothing more than thoughts. Kabril never mentioned such a thing occurring with Rayna. It had to just be a coincidence.

She took several steps away from him, adjusting herself along the way. "Where are you staying?"

Close to you.

He regarded her with caution for she looked much like she was about to take flight. As if that were even possible. "In the area. Why?" he said coolly.

"Is there a number I can reach you at?" Her gaze drifted towards the barn door. "Please don't leave town until I've had a chance to—"

"You two coming?" Bailey asked, opening the door.

Paige forced a smile to her face. "I am. Sachin just remembered he has another appointment. He won't be able to join us for lunch. Maybe another time."

Allowing her to think he'd leave for now was best. He nodded and left Paige in the stables with Bailey. The minute Sachin was around the side of the structure he removed his clothing quickly and shoved it behind a barrel. A sharp pinching, followed closely by a feeling of freedom swept over him as he shifted form into that of a hawk. He selected the smallest size he could, which was still considerably bigger than the hawks that frequented the human realm. He took flight and circled the stables, watching as Paige and Bailey emerged from within. He hovered high in the air, ever mindful of where they were and what they were doing.

Chapter Eight

PAIGE TRIED AND FAILED TO SHAKE THE feeling she was being watched. She sat on the deck of the main house, picking at the food Bailey's mother had prepared.

"You feeling all right?" Bailey asked.

"I'm fine. Why?"

"You've hardly said more than a few words and I don't think you've heard a word I've said."

She set her fork down. "I heard you."

He gave her an amused look. "Oh, really? Then where did I suggest we take our honeymoon?"

She gulped. Okay, maybe she hadn't been listening to him. "Someplace romantic?" she asked, hopeful she could skate on such a thin answer.

Bailey snickered. "If your feet are getting cold, I could warm them for you." The innuendo wasn't lost on her. "I have to get back to work, but later tonight I could warm you up real nice."

"Tonight is date night." She winked. "You're not trying to get out of having to take me out on the town, are you?"

A mock gasp came from him. "I would never."

"Right."

He blushed. "Didn't hurt to try to get out of dancing, right?"

"No." She giggled. "I guess it didn't, but you're still meeting me for date night. Like it or not. And, Bailey, what if we waited a little while to get married."

He began to toy with his paper plate. "Are you telling me you want out of this?"

"No, I'm just trying to avoid rushing into anything. I'd like some more time."

"If it's time you need, Paige, it's time you'll have." He kissed the back of her hand. "I want you to be happy."

She wanted to be happy too, but Paige knew now that Bailey wasn't the man who could make that happen. It pained her to know in the end he would be hurt if she dared to give in to the pull Sachin seemed to have over her.

"Penny for your thoughts."

She took his hand and rubbed it over her cheek. "You're a good man, Bailey. Too good for me."

Bailey slid around to her side of the table and pressed his lips to her cheek. The feel of him so close normally made her crave his affection. Not now. No, now she couldn't resist glancing towards an over-sized oak tree that sat near the deck. Something was watching her, or someone.

Sachin.

If what she suspected was true, he very well could be near and she would be none the wiser. Paige held tight to her emotions, unwilling to let on about her fears and suspicions. Bailey would never understand. He'd think she was crazy and he could try to harm the people she cared most about.

Bailey leaned in, his mouth greeting

hers. He wasn't the man she wanted to spend her life with, but he was the only one who was reliable. The next best thing. She gave in and pressed her lips to his. Closing her eyes, Paige opened her mouth as Bailey swept his tongue in. He moaned and she tipped her head.

He inched closer and Paige squirmed, adjusting to get comfortable.

The sound of a bird screeching jarred her from their kiss just in time for a massive amount of bird poop to land on Bailey's head.

"Ahh." He shot up and off the table, his eyes to the sky. "What the hell?"

Paige grabbed a handful of napkins and lifted them. "Here." She looked up, positive she was not only being watched, but that whatever was there was now very pleased with itself. "That must have been some bird."

Bailey finished wiping himself and tossed the napkins aside. "I think I pissed off the bird people."

She froze. "W-what?"

He laughed. "You know, the bird

people. I'm sure you've heard the towns-people go on and on about the legends surrounding the area."

She wasn't born and bred there, but rather an outsider who tried to stay out of the mix. "No. What rumors?"

"That half men, half birds guard this area, watching over it and protecting it from evil." He gave a lighthearted snort. "And shitting on the local sheriff."

Paige paled, her heart pounding. Flashes of a man with wings filled her mind. They mixed with images of her mother and her mother's boyfriend. She covered her mouth as scenes from that horrible night crashed into her mind, making her remember things better left forgotten. She could vaguely remember Sachin being there. He'd helped her to safety; that much she remembered. Small glimpses of him descending from the night sky, long brown wings extended before curling into him and disappearing, filled her mind. Paige shook her head.

It's not true. It can't be. I've lost my mind. That's it. I'm going crazy.

But what if she wasn't? She had to know. Could the legends be true, and if they were, was Sachin one of these half men, half birds? If he was, the repercussions would be massive. She fumbled through the basket and found wet wipes. She held the package out to Bailey who took two. "Tell me more about the local legends."

Bailey sat and proceeded to finish cleaning himself. "I can't believe Sarah hasn't told you all about them. Her father was a big believer." He pointed towards the mountains. "He used to tell everyone they came from up there. That they flew over his ranch often and that they were warriors of good. Hell, I even remember stories about her father going down on his knees in the middle of his field to give thanks to them for protecting his baby girl."

Paige let out a nervous chuckle. "And what do you think? Do you believe men can change into birds?"

Bailey's cell phone rang, interrupting their talk. He groaned as he glanced at the caller ID. "It's the station. I have to take this."

"I understand." And she did. More than she wanted to. She didn't need Bailey to confirm what she was fast suspecting to be true. Sachin was no mere mortal man. Any doubts she had could be addressed by looking no further than her home.

Glancing up, she spotted an oversized hawk perched on a branch near the edge of the house. She tilted her head and lifted a hand to shield her face from direct sun. A familiar set of silver eyes stared back at her from the high branch. Air swooshed out of her lungs as she clutched the side of the table. Every suspicion she'd ever had about Sachin rushed over her.

"No."

The bird nodded its head as if answering her.

She shook so hard the table moved. "I'm officially insane."

No. You are not.

"Sachin?" she asked, staring up at the bird, sure she'd heard Sachin's voice in her head.

Chapter Nine

PAIGE LEANED AGAINST THE JUKEBOX. THE hairs on the back of her neck rose and she twisted enough to see across the crowded bar. A set of silver eyes stared back at her. The remembered feel of his caresses only hours before left Paige drawing in a deep breath, trying to calm her nerves. He was too much. Too intense, and the way he watched her like she was a meal to be feasted upon nearly did her in.

She scanned the bar for signs of Bailey. He still wasn't there. With Sachin's return she was foolish for thinking she could still lead a normal life.

In the back of her mind she'd known Sachin would come for her, that he wasn't a man to take no for an answer. For some reason Paige had thought she might be able to convince him to go, to just let her live in peace.

There is no peace from our kind of bond, ta'konima.

Reaching up, she tried to block his voice from intruding in her mind. It was official, she was going insane, imagining the man she loved speaking in her head.

I too denied my ability to hear you, he said, his mouth never moving. *I was wrong. So are you.*

Paige swallowed hard and rubbed her arms. *This isn't happening. It's not real. I'm having another nightmare.*

Sachin shook his head. No. *This is not a nightmare, Paige.*

"Sachin?" A soft moan came out as she tried and failed to deny he was communicating with her telepathically.

You should rejoice. A bad-boy grin spread over his face. *It means you are indeed sane.*

Yes. She shivered. *But what does that mean you are, Sachin, because I don't think you're human.*

There was a slip in his step but he recovered quickly, walking towards her. The crowd seemed to part as if by magik, allowing him to pass through them untouched.

Great. He's not only more than a man, he's some kind of god.

I'm no god, ta'konima.

Says you.

A rich, deep laugh echoed in her head, signaling he was in control of the situation, not her.

As it should be.

She leveled her gaze on him, allowing it to harden. "No more," she mouthed.

Not enough, ta'konima. *You are mine and I will not stand idly by and allow you to marry another. You will pick me.*

"Or else?" she asked, her voice low.

There is no or else, Paige. You will pick me. I merely stated a fact.

She rolled her eyes and a smile curved her mouth. He came to a stop in front of her.

Paige knew she should be afraid of him on some level but she wasn't. She'd never trusted anyone more in her life. "Fancy meeting you here."

He winked. "I was in the neighborhood."

"Just flyin' through?" she asked, the need to make light of what she'd suspected surfacing. What she had to ask him.

Sachin put his large hands on her hips and they nearly touched around her waist. He gave a gentle squeeze before jerking her against the expanse of his chest. Air whooshed from her lungs and he laughed, clearly amused by his actions. "My apologies. There are times I forget my own strength."

"Yeah, right," she teased.

The music changed, the beat slowing. Sachin swayed their bodies to the rhythm. He ground his pelvis against her and she hissed at the feel of his erection, thick, long and even bigger than she remembered. She should push him away. She was with Bailey now. Instead, she clung tighter to him. It made no sense, but nothing about Sachin ever did.

Paige wasn't sure how long they

danced, their bodies pressed close together. Sachin led her from the dance floor, towards the front door. He pushed it open with ease and the cool night air bit at her skin. With as hot as he made her feel, the air was much needed.

Sachin dragged her around the corner of the bar and pressed her against the exterior wall. It was cold and her body felt feverish in comparison. She grunted and grabbed hold of his shirt collar. Her breath quickened as he bent, devouring her mouth. This was wrong but felt right for so many reasons. Stopping wasn't an option. It didn't matter that they were in public and anyone could walk past and see. That only added to the thrill.

With some careful maneuvering, Sachin had her lifted off the ground with her legs wrapped around his waist in record time. The hard press of his cock reminded Paige what was at stake. To give in to him again could be her undoing. She barely survived him leaving before. She wouldn't make it if he did it again.

I won't leave you, ta'konima.

He surged forward, rubbing himself against her mound. A moan escaped her lips and Paige knew the man before her held her captive with desire.

Sachin swept his tongue around her mouth. His hand dipped into her blouse and he cupped a breast, kneading it with one hand while he yanked her miniskirt up with the other.

"You are not wearing panties," he said, breaking their kiss momentarily.

"I know."

He stiffened. "Did you plan on being with your sheriff tonight, Paige?" The malice in his voice was evident.

A piece of her wanted to lie and tell him that she did intend to be with someone else just to spite him, but she couldn't. Truth be told, deep down she'd known it was Sachin she'd be with.

He didn't wait for her answer. He shoved his body hard against hers as he lifted her skirt above her hips. A feral smile eased over his mouth but he continued to kiss her. He ran a finger along her cleft and dipped it into her pussy.

Tipping her head back, Paige felt her body contract around his finger. She knew she was wet, drenched even. He made her this way. He added a second finger and ripped at her blouse. Buttons popped off and then he broke her bra open. An excited cry echoed in the air around them and it took Paige a second to realize she was the one who made the noise.

She shoved her hands down, going straight for the front of his pants. Sachin chuckled into her mouth, his kisses so erotic they pushed her near her peak. Liquid warmth oozed from her.

Freeing his cock, she bit at his lower lip and he growled, making her tingle. She stroked his velvety-smooth shaft. There were so many things she needed to talk about with him but nothing seemed important enough to stop the carnal passion flaring between them.

He lifted her higher and speared her on the end of his cock. She cried out, digging her fingernails into his shoulders. He thrusts were long and deep. His lower abdomen rubbed against her clit just right, sending waves of pleasure through her. Her inner thighs tightened and Paige knew she was on the verge of coming.

Clenching her teeth, she rode him hard and fast. His movements were strong and powerful, pushing her into the wall to the point she thought for sure something would break.

Her climax struck and she writhed against him, holding him tight. "S-Sachin."

Chapter Ten

THE SOUND OF HIS NAME FALLING FROM Paige's lips was heaven. Sachin put his palms against the building and fucked her with all he had. She took everything he offered, crying out again as another orgasm went through her. The walls of her pussy grasped his cock, pulling him nearer to finishing. Sachin bit at his inner cheek, grounding himself, needing to prolong the pleasure as much as possible.

The scent of her arousal drove him mad. He barely kept hold of his pending shift, channeling the energy instead into pumping in and out of Paige. Animalistic grunts and growls came from them and Sachin could smell blood. He knew Paige had scratched him open and he was proud of his mate's fierceness.

Reaching down, he used his fingers to massage her clit. She screamed his name and slammed her head back into the wall repeatedly. It was then Sachin was sure he'd passed on his immortal strength and healing to her. A human would have damaged themselves. Paige was unharmed.

"Ohmygod," she panted. "There. There."

"Tell me what you want." His voice was harsh but it was only due to his strain to keep from coming.

"I want you." Her brown gaze locked on him. "Only you."

Her slit held firm to him, seeming to pull him back into her womb, hungry for his seed. Sachin's balls tightened and he let out a battle cry as he allowed his release to finally come to fruition.

Paige swiveled her hips on him and clenched her pussy, milking his cock thoroughly. She smiled, her cheeks flushed and her eyes lust filled. "Mmm, that was…nice."

"Nice?" He arched a brow in question.

She giggled and planted a chaste kiss on his lips. "Perfect?"

He shook his head, wanting more from her.

"The best I've ever had?"

Sachin grinned. "Getting closer."

She wiggled, and their combined juices leaked from their joined bodies. "Tell me what you want to hear."

"That you love me," he confessed.

Her lips met his and the kiss caused him to harden once more. When she drew back, her gaze was dark. "Sachin, I've loved you from the day I met you. It's you who doesn't love me."

He rooted himself deep within her and cupped her neck with one hand. "Do not presume to know how I feel, Paige. I confessed my feelings for you when we first joined all those months ago."

She appeared puzzled. "No, you didn't."

Tugging on her jaw with his thumb,

Sachin forced her mouth open and slid his tongue around it. "Mmm, yes, I did. I called you *ta'konima*... It means my love."

She bit his tongue, staying just this side of painful. It drove him onward, making him burn with a need to find bliss in her again. She was his ball of flames. Wild. Untamed. His Firecracker.

Spearing into her, Sachin lost control, taking her harder than he should have. Stopping himself wasn't an option and Paige countered each movement with grace. She held onto him, kissing his mouth, neck, shoulder—whatever she could. His mind numbed to all but the feel of her cunt around his shaft. Another orgasm crashed through him just as Paige hit the brink as well. She trembled against him, kissing him softly as she cried in his arms.

Fearful he'd harmed her, Sachin withdrew. "Paige?"

"I'm fine." She cried harder. "I just can't believe you're really here. That you're back. I keep thinking I'll close my eyes and you'll be gone." She stared at him. "That you'll simply fly away."

Fly.

The word had been dropped more than once since his return. He wondered how much Paige really knew about him. Had she regained her memories of the night her mother died? Did she remember seeing him toss the enemy into a tree without remorse and with superhuman strength? Did she view him as a monster?

Paige shook her head and caressed his lower lip with her finger. "Not a monster, Sachin. And no, my memory of that night is still broken. I remember bits and pieces, but you've helped me connect the dots." She exhaled and put her forehead to his chest. "You saved my life. You protected me."

"I was too late to save your mother. I'm sorry. I should have been faster. I should have—"

"Shhh." She put the tips of her fingers to his mouth. "You saved me. Why?"

He opened his mouth to answer her and

was interrupted when someone cleared their throat. He sniffed the air and recognized the sheriff's scent. Sachin locked gazes with Paige. "I'm sorry. This was not how I wanted things to end between you and your —" he almost said human but refrained "—sheriff. But trust me when I say it will end."

"What?" Paige's eyes widened as she glanced over the top of Sachin's shoulder. She drew in a sharp breath and pushed at him, trying to get down. "Oh God. I… Bailey. This isn't… Bailey."

Sachin refused to let Paige down. He kept her pinned to the wall, already knowing the sheriff had seen them in the act of coupling. There was no shame in taking one's mate. It mattered not that the sheriff had asked Paige to marry him. She was his and he would not share.

"Sachin, let me down."

"He will not forgive you for this," he whispered. "Let him walk away, Paige."

"No. I have to talk to him. I have to make this right." She covered her mouth with her hand. "I cheated on him. Why?" She smacked Sachin across the face.

Ignoring the sting, Sachin stared down at her. "You can blame me if you wish, but the truth is we were created for one another, Paige. Your body recognizes mine and craves mine as mine does yours."

Paige looked past him. "Sachin, he's gone. Bailey's gone and I didn't get to talk to him."

Content, he set her down. She kicked him in the shin. Much to his surprise, it hurt. He blinked. "Paige?"

She kicked him again, this time in the knee and he staggered. He barely managed to get his cock back into his pants before Paige was trying to do it again. He caught her leg and held it gently.

"No more."

"You," she growled, "are an overbearing, bossy, know-it-all jerk!"

He grinned. "Thank you."

A few rather well-placed slaps later and Paige seemed to be under control. She smoothed her hair back and cast him an uneasy look. "You should have let me talk to him."

"And you shouldn't have agreed to be with another man," he said without remorse.

She baulked. "What? Was I supposed to wait around forever, hoping you'd show up, when you vanished without a trace?"

He hadn't really thought of it like that, but even so, yes. He flashed a wicked smile at her, knowing it would set her temper off again. "Yes. You were."

"Ooo." She stomped on his foot. "You…you…horse's ass!"

He snickered.

When she didn't laugh but rather looked to be on the verge of tears, he sobered. "Paige."

A lone tear fell down her cheek. "You stripped me of my innocence and you left me alone, thinking I'd done something wrong. That I'd somehow displeased you." She ran a hand through her thick hair and stared upwards at the night sky. "Why, Sachin?"

He took hold of her arms and tried to coax her into wrapping them around his waist. She resisted. "*Ta'konima*, you've never displeased me. You were too much for me. Too glorious to be with that I couldn't hide it anymore."

Confused, Paige looked at him, needing answers to old questions. "Couldn't hide what?"

"What I am."

"And what, exactly, are you?" she asked, her voice as shaky as her legs felt.

"More than a man, Paige, but I believe you know this to be true. I think," he pressed his palm to her chest, "your heart told you so long ago."

He was right, but that was beside the point. She needed to hear from his lips what he was. "Sachin, please."

"Not now. Soon. I promise."

A sinking feeling centered in the pit of her stomach. She'd given up everything she'd worked so hard to build with Bailey for Sachin to continue with his same old game. What was she thinking?

She pressed against him. "I have to go. I need space. Time to think."

His lips formed a thin line. "Time to go to him?"

"He deserves an explanation."

"And what will you tell him? Will you tell him that you offered yourself to me, practically begging me to take your innocence? That the minute I came back into your life, you surrendered to me, allowing me to fuck you against a wall, in public, for all to see?"

"I wish you had stayed gone!" Beyond hurt by Sachin's words, Paige blinked back tears and shoved him as hard as she could. She suspected he moved back on his own because she was nowhere near strong enough to move him.

She walked away as fast as her heels would take her, refusing to look at him.

Chapter Eleven

PAIGE WENT TO THE DOOR THINKING THE knocking in the middle of the night was from Sachin. When she opened it to find Bailey standing there, her heart sank. He looked tired, his eyes were red and his hair was a mess.

"Can I come in?" he asked.

Sarah was a light sleeper and Paige didn't want to wake her. She grabbed a blanket from the edge of the chair and wrapped it around herself like a shawl. "I'll come out."

Bailey stepped back, letting her pass.

The cold porch stung her bare feet. "I tried to call you."

"I know. I wasn't ready to talk just yet."

She eyed him closely. "But you are now?"

Nodding, he sat on the railing of the porch. "How much do you know about this guy, Paige?"

Fear slammed through her. "Why? Did something happen to him?"

"I didn't shoot him if that's what you're asking. I thought about it." Bailey let out a low whistle. "A lot. But I didn't. I also didn't find any records of him existing."

"You ran a check on him?" she asked, unable to believe her ears.

Bailey shrugged nonchalantly. "Someone has to watch out for you, Paige." He appeared nervous. "There is something I found though, some talk around town, involving your mysterious *lover*," he said the word with venom. "He's been seen in the area before, around the time of your mother's death."

She grabbed hold of the edge of the railing to keep from falling as Bailey's unvoiced accusations struck her head-on.

"Sachin had nothing to do with Hank murdering my mother."

"But did he have something to do with Hank's death?"

She wanted to lie eloquently but Bailey knew her too well. She kept her eyes cast downward. "No."

"Paige, you can tell me. Was it self defense?"

She couldn't answer him. To do so would lead to too many questions for Sachin, and Paige knew he couldn't answer them. Not to Bailey's satisfaction.

He grabbed her wrist. "Talk to me. I deserve an answer."

"Are we still talking about the same question?" she asked, jerking her wrist free from his grasp. "I never meant to hurt you, Bailey."

"But you did."

"Paige?" Sachin stepped from the shadows.

Bailey's hand went to his sidearm and Paige's eyes widened. Sachin appeared amused by it all. He waved a hand in the air. "You will leave here and never remember meeting me. You will move on from Paige, find someone else to care for, and be happy she has found her soul mate."

Paige stared between the two men and then burst into a fit of laughter. She clutched her stomach. "Oh, no way will that ever work."

Bailey walked past her, looking dazed. He headed straight for his car and never glanced back.

She turned to face Sachin with her mouth wide open. He pressed her jaw shut and laughed. "I am a man of many talents, wife."

"Wife?" She rubbed her temples. "You're also a man who has a lot of explaining to do."

"I'd like to show you something first." Yanking his shirt over his head, he took her breath away.

"Sachin, I've seen all of you already. It's what got me into trouble to start with."

"Close your eyes."

She obeyed and heard a flapping noise.

"Open them."

A wave of dizziness swept through Paige as she stared at the man she loved, his wings spread wide. "You're a…oh my," she said before swaying.

Sachin was suddenly there, pulling her to his chest. "Are you well?"

"You're a bird man." Paige tried to think of something profound to offer but came up empty. "Whoa."

Sachin's nervous chuckle seemed to set her at ease but she wasn't sure why. It did remind her of the man she'd come to love, helping to tone down the very real fact that he was more than met the eye.

She reached out to touch one of his wings but stopped just shy of making contact. "Will I hurt you?"

His silver gaze lit with amusement. "No, but you will run the risk of making me want to be buried deep within you." He licked his lower lip. "When a *Buteos Regalis* male has his wings caressed by his female…his mate…they tell me it is extremely erotic. I would not know—yet."

Paige jerked her hand back and Sachin laughed long and loud. "What? I've seen how insatiable you are when not getting your wings stroked." She blushed. "That sounded dirty, didn't it?"

He stiffened and stared up at the night sky. "Paige," his voice was low, "go into the house and do not come out, regardless what you hear."

Fear slammed through her. "What's wrong?" She looked up too, trying to see whatever threat he obviously did, but found none.

"Go!" Sachin shoved her towards the door. "I did not think I would be followed. If they find you, they will use you against me and—"

He didn't need to finish his sentence. Paige understood that whatever Sachin was afraid of would not be something she'd want to tangle with. Nodding, she turned and rushed into the house. She glanced back to find Sachin gone.

———

SACHIN TOOK FLIGHT, the smell of his enemies surrounding him. He knew there was a risk of drawing attention to the farm by frequenting it, but he'd been doing it for so many years he'd grown careless. He'd been foolish to believe he could actually leave the war behind and take leave.

The battle cry of the Falcos filled the night air and Sachin cursed himself for being unarmed. A flash of silver reflected in the moonlight as one of his enemies dove at him, blade extended. He dodged the strike, only just.

Another Falco attacked, this one from his right. Sachin struck out, slamming his fist into the man's face. Yet another came at him and soon Sachin found himself grossly outnumbered and unarmed.

He locked gazes with a man he'd met in battle before. He was a general for the Falcos and notorious for his cruelty to the women of Sachin's race. The idea of the bastard getting to Paige in any way gave Sachin the boost he needed to fight on.

Something sharp pierced his side and he glanced down to find the end of a sword stuck straight through him. Time seemed to slow as the sounds of gunfire surrounded him. The enemy lurched back, one by one, and Sachin cupped his side, cutting his hands on the blade as he tumbled towards the ground. He struck the ground hard, driving the sword through his body more, impaling himself fully.

Paige screamed and appeared above him with a rifle in her hand. Sarah was there as well, equally as armed. Sarah touched Paige's shoulder. "Calm yourself or you're of no use to him. We can handle this."

Sachin reached for Sarah. "Not...safe. If they find...either of you...they'll..."

Sarah gave him a stern, mothering look. "If I shot you in the head, could you get up and attack me?"

Puzzled, he shook his head. A wound such as that to the head would be fatal even for a shifter such as himself. "No."

She grinned. "Then rest assured, boy, they won't be bothering us again. When my girl and I aim, we aim to kill, not to maim. What's the sense of that? Now, let's get you onto your side. Paige, get my medical bag."

Paige ran off towards the house and Sarah touched Sachin's cheek tenderly. "We'll get you fixed up and then you'll take her far from here. You'll take her home with you and start a family."

He did a long blink for his acknowledgement, liking her plan for their future.

Sarah tipped her head. "And you'll be sure to bring her and any grandbabies I get from the two of you to visit me often. Understood?"

He laughed and instantly regretted it as pain shot through him. "Yes, ma'am." As he stared up at Sarah, he knew everything would indeed be all right.

Epilogue

SACHIN WRAPPED HIS ARMS AROUND HIS wife and held her close to him. It was hard to believe even after close to a year together that she was well and truly his. Her stomach was swollen with a life their love had created. She was due soon, at least according to the healers. He hoped to have a son or sons as was the case with Kabril. The king's triplets were pushing one year old and kept him on his toes. Each time Paige and Sachin saw the boys, they found themselves both excited and nervous about the coming birth of their child.

Often Kabril was left exhausted and Sachin wondered if he had the energy to deal with *any* little ones, let alone three. Still, the idea that his love for Paige had resulted in something so precious and sacred to his people made any doubts he had ease away.

Paige put her hands over his and leaned against him. "I still can't get over how beautiful it is here."

She'd lived among his people, in his realm, for almost a year, and hearing she still found beauty in it pleased him deeply. It had been difficult for her to get used to the loss of certain things she'd enjoyed greatly on Earth, but she'd found other things to occupy her time. Paige was prized among his people for her healing skills with not only their animals, but their shifted forms as well. She spent afternoons aiding the castle healers.

She twisted in his arms, her stomach forcing him back slightly. Wisely, he didn't comment on it but rather cupped her face and planted a kiss upon her lips. "I have to leave with Lazar soon. Promise to stay out of trouble while I'm gone."

She smiled. "Have I thanked you yet

for offering to bring Sarah here for the birth of our baby?"

"Yes, but," he waggled his brows, "I can think of other things you can do to show how grateful you are."

Paige gave him a light shove and laughed. "I can't see my toes. We aren't doing anything."

"Nothing?" He stuck out his bottom lip.

She cast a scolding look in his direction. "You're insatiable."

"I know," he said proudly. "You wouldn't have me any other way."

"You're right but..." Paige bent quickly, grabbing her stomach and crying out in pain.

Sachin caught hold of her arms. "Paige?"

"Baby. Now."

"What? No. Not now. We're not ready yet. I haven't finished assembling the nursery and Sarah is not here yet. And..."

Seizing hold of his hand, Paige clawed it as she glared up at him. "Sachin!"

He took a deep breath but it did nothing to calm him. "Yes?"

"It's time. Get Rayna."

"But…"

She looked down as water gushed down her inner thighs. Sachin blinked, staring at his wife and knowing she was in pain. He took a tiny step back and the room began to spin.

———

"SACHIN."

Sachin lifted his head and stared around, unsure how it was he came to be in the hallway. Kabril stood over him with a mug of ale in his hand. "What happened?"

Kabril grinned. "Your wife went into labor and you, my trusted advisor and head of my guards, passed out cold."

Sachin pushed to his feet and rushed his chamber-room door. His heart felt as if it were lodged in his throat as he entered the room. Rayna backed away from the edge of the bed and Paige came into view.

Her cheeks were rosy and her auburn hair was tousled. In her arms lay two tiny bundles. They were motionless and silent. Panic welled in him and his gaze snapped to Rayna. "They're well?"

She winked. "They're fine. Mommy is a bit tired though."

He went to Paige's side and bent, kissing the top of her head. He stared down at the babies. "My sons are so tiny."

Paige snorted. "Uh, you try squeezing them out, and for your information, we have daughters."

Daughters? He leaned forward and uncovered the child on the right. Sure enough, it lacked the equipment necessary to be his son. The temperature of the room seemed to spike and he locked gazes with his wife. "We have baby girls?"

She bit her lower lip and nodded. It was clear to see she was trying not to laugh at him. "I can't wait until they're old enough to date. I want to see the look on their faces when you—"

"Date?" Sachin swayed, suddenly

feeling sick to his stomach. "No. It will not happen. Absolutely, positively not."

Rayna laughed at Paige. "You win."

A sly smile spread over Paige's face. "Do I know my man or what?" She glanced at Sachin. "Honey, if you feel faint you should—"

The room seemed to spin and the next thing Sachin knew, Kabril was by his side, laughing from the gut.

THE END

NOTE TO READERS: Author recommends reading Master of the Hunt next for max reading enjoyment. Buy Link for Master of the Hunt

Complimentary Material

The Raven Books' Complimentary
Material
The following material is free of charge. It
will never affect the price of your book.

Sacred Places (Druid Series) by Mandy
M. Roth

Sometimes fated love requires some good old-fash-
ioned magikal meddling.

Coyle O'Caha, a seven-hundred-year-
old immortal, druid sorcerer, is a famed
warrior among his kind and a legendary
ladies' man—but that doesn't mean he
hasn't spent his life looking for his soul-
mate. That one woman who will make him

feel whole. When Deri walks into his seaside pub, clearly running from something or someone, it's all he can do to not sweep her off her feet and claim her right then and there. It's as if the goddess is mocking him. Not only is his mate immune to his charms *and* his magik, she's human.

Deri Sullivan's new boss has a Scottish lilt that makes her knees weak. The problem is he's a certified ladies' man. And she's sworn off those types—for good. If only she could stop dreaming about him in ways that would make any girl blush. See, she has a secret, and even if she wanted to let Coyle into her bed, she couldn't actually let him into her life. Witches and humans simply don't mix.

Expert from Sacred Places by Mandy M. Roth

Coyle O'Caha bent over his woodworking bench and continued to carve into a piece of oak he'd been toying with for several weeks now. He disliked when he came across oak trees being cut down, and often bought them in bulk to avoid them going to waste.

Oak was special to his people—the druids. Humans held little regard for oak in the way they should. Truth be told, humans did not care for much, other than themselves. He was not a fan of them but understood they were a necessary evil. An evil he was charged with protecting.

Stupid rules.

He sighed. There were days he often wondered if the goddess selected right when sending him to be birthed to a family of druid sorcerers and then tasking them with overseeing humans' safety as well as the training of other magiks.

He didn't mind magiks so much.

Though, more and more the new batches of witches coming through his doors for guidance held less and less respect for the craft and for its roots. They merely sought power for the sake of power. Those types almost always ended up going bad—souring and becoming something Coyle, his brothers and cousins hunted.

It had been a month or more since the last dark sorcerer had surfaced. The O'Caha boys dispatched him quickly, ending his life and harnessing his dark magik to keep it from reentering the ether and causing issues later. The dark sorcerer had more bluster than actual power. Guess he should have waited to go to the dark side before he started issuing threats and trying to be a badass, because he'd not had the juice to back his threats. Most threats were easy to deal with considering the ages of the O'Caha boys. Though, every once in a while one would crop up who took some real effort.

Korey, his first cousin and best friend, had just returned from a hunt for a dark sorcerer like that—one who took a toll on the person or people hunting him. Korey had gotten a little banged up but was fine. The same couldn't be said for their cousin Gordon. He'd already suffered at the hands of demons and was paying the price. All the O'Caha men held guilt over

Gordon. They each felt as though they'd failed him in some fashion.

And they had.

He'd been brutally attacked and held captive for months by a dark sorcerer who had turned to the ways of the vampires—the blood drinkers. Gordon had not come out the other side of the ordeal the same as he'd gone in.

Who would?

Gordon now was also considered a vampire, though none of the O'Caha boys would ever dream of hunting him. The damn *eejit* thought himself a danger to mankind and was doing a damn fine job of trying to end himself. The fool had no idea that the good-hearted man he'd once been still remained. That the blood drinker side of him did not rule him.

Couldn't get it through Gordon's thick skull, though.

Another O'Caha faulty trait.

Stubbornness.

For more information about these

titles and other bestselling Mandy M. Roth titles please visit www.MandyRoth.com

A King's Ransom by Reagan Hawk
(pen name of Mandy M. Roth)
Book One in the Masters of Pleasure Series

On a quest to find his brother, King Kritan of Katarius on the planet of Panucia finds himself ambushed, beaten, tortured and then sold to fight in the arena games. The people of Tamonius—his rival kingdom—condone slavery, take public sex to new lows and try to turn a profit off anything they can. Nothing can change his hatred for everything Tamonius… That is, until he meets the most breathtakingly beautiful woman he's ever laid eyes upon. Surina of the House of Argyros, daughter to a powerful senator, stirs the beast within him, making it want to lay claim to her as badly as the man does.

Free or not, Kritan is a master of seduction, and has selected Surina as his newest prey. But this virginal beauty has secrets of her own—ones that change everything. And destiny just might have the last laugh.

To find out more about these books or to read other books from The Raven Books visit www.TheRavenBooks.com

Master of the Hunt Blurb

Master of the Hunt
Book three in the King of Prey series.

When the oracle warns Prince Aeson that his future mate is in the human realm and is in great danger, he wastes no time going in search of her. Problem is, he has no idea who he's looking for. He's never met her and the oracle couldn't give him anything more than small clues as to who she is and where she might be.

Sent to one of his favorite hangouts—a sex club—Aeson is stunned when a beauty shows up on the arm of another man, a man void of emotion. He senses trouble surrounding her and something else—something that marks her as his. He doesn't care if she is or isn't the woman the oracle told him about, she's the woman he wants. Anyone who dares to stand in his way will feel his wrath and, before the night is out, she'll feel exactly what it's like to be taken by a prince.

Click to buy Master of the Hunt **today!**

Excerpt: Mast of the Hunt

CHAPTER ONE

ACCIPITRIDAE REALM, BUTEOS REGALIS MAIN castle...

AESON STEPPED BACK, allowing his nephews to run past him, each babbling about something he could not understand. Their father, the king and Aeson's eldest brother, chased behind them, appearing winded. In the nearly four hundred years he'd known him, Aeson couldn't recall a time when Kabril looked so unraveled. His duplicate in looks in every way, it was as though Aeson were seeing himself in such a situation.

The sight was sobering indeed.

"Kabril, you are showing your age," Aeson said, enjoying goading his brother as often as he could.

"I am two minutes older than you," Kabril replied. He motioned to his triplets, who were pushing the age of three. "I know naught how our father did it. Eight sons." He looked horrified by the idea. "They are my heart and joy, but brother, they never tire. It is the equivalent to one laying siege to the castle nonstop."

Chuckling, Aeson nodded. "So I see."

"Brother, the moons hold great pull over them. When the moons are full, I swear my sons sleep not."

Aeson laughed. Four moons orbited their planet. One of the moons was large enough to be seen during daylight hours. Often, the moons were attributed when madness, or in this case, too much energy came into play. "I do not believe for a moment they are subject to the moons' pull. They are merely young boys —fledglings—Kabril. We are old. They are not. It stands to reason they would have more energy than us. It is good to hear the sounds of children in the king-dom. For too long it was void of such noises."

Kabril motioned to the nanny charged with overseeing the boys before turning to face his brother. "No word of new births among our people has reached me. To date, only Rayna and I, and Sachin and his mate Paige have been successful. You know, Rayna believes we should consult the Oracle on the matter. She thinks it may provide valuable insight into what our next move should be."

Aeson cringed at the mention of the prophecy giving globe. From an early age he'd learned to both fear and stand in awe of the oracle's power. It was often consulted on matters associated with the gods or destiny. Kabril, unlike their father, wasn't superstitious. It made him a better leader in Aeson's opinion than their father had been, not that he'd been a bad one. "And I say you decree that all your loyal subjects must procreate like mad," Aeson said.

Kabril rolled his eyes. "Still chasing

skirts in the taverns throughout the realm?"

With a sly smile, Aeson rubbed his stubble-covered jaw. "Not in this realm, brother. I'm unsure a maiden exists here that I've not bedded. Earth is another matter altogether."

That caused his brother to stumble over seemingly nothing. "You? The famed lover of women of our kind and hater of all things human, now seeks out the beds of human women?"

"No. Not beds. But I do enjoy chaining them to walls and having my way with them," he replied. His cock hardened at the very thought of it. He did so enjoy women of all sizes and shapes. And he very much enjoyed taking them in different ways. "Did you know they have taverns or rather sex clubs, as they call them, devoted to that very thing? They rival our torture chambers and the women there line up for it, wanting to be punished by a man's hand before being thoroughly pleasured." He motioned with his hands, framing an invisible woman with exaggerated measurements. He then pumped his hips in midair, simulating fucking said woman.

"If my wife hears you speak of such things," Kabril leaned in, "and of demeaning human women in such a way, she will skin you alive. She may be human but she is something to be feared, brother."

Aeson tossed his head back and laughed. Rayna certainly was a fiery woman. She kept his brother in line nicely and brought out the best in him. He clasped his brother's shoulder. "Should I find one such as she, mayhap I would wish to chain her to my bed for I am not foolish enough to think I am immune to all women's charms."

"Do you not wish for a family, Aeson?" There was something off in Kabril's voice. "Do you not wish for love and happiness?"

He glanced in the direction his nephews had run off in. "I do not wish for such a thing." It was a bold faced lie. One he was sure his brother saw through with ease.

"Because you have no desire for one or

because you desire one so much that you fear it might not come true?"

His brother knew him well. Not only did they look much alike—nearly identical to those who didn't know them well—they tended to think on the same terms too. Though, Kabril had always taken things more seriously than Aeson had. Mainly because Kabril, as firstborn son, had to. Second to the throne in a family that was close-knit, Aeson saw no point in worrying over kingly matters when the odds of him ever having the throne were slim. Even Keonae, the youngest of the triplets, saw no need to trouble himself with the day-to-day trials and tribulations of running a kingdom. For reasons too dark to dwell upon, Keonae now resided permanently within the human realm—a place Aeson found himself drawn to more and more as of late.

Kabril entered the Great Hall and Aeson followed closely behind. Chains of gold hung suspended from the high ceilings. Open saucers with floating wicks were upon the ends of each, illuminating the vast room.

Aeson's brother took a seat on his throne. There was a reflective mixture in a bowl sitting to the left of the throne. Aeson knew it was used to help divine the future, something Kabril rarely did on his own, leaving the seers to do so for him.

Kabril eased back in his chair, his fingers skimming over the carved hawks in the dark wood. "Brother, it was not that long ago I found myself in your position. Wanting to deny what the Oracle had set forth for me."

"Good thing we have yet to consult it for me then, yes?" A nervous chortle broke free of him.

Pressing his mouth in a thin line, Kabril motioned for one of the attendants. "Bring the Oracle."

"What?" Aeson paled. "Kabril, no."

The attendants hurried off, nearly knocking over one of the suspended oil lamps in their haste to please the king.

His brother smiled. "Ah, it would appear you are too late."

Grunting, Aeson gave his brother a pensive look. "I have no wish to hear talk of things that may not come to pass. Worse yet, it tell me I'm to wed a woman with a hunched back or who is missing her teeth."

"Think it likely?" Kabril questioned. "We have such an abundance of them? We may not have many females in our realm but none are as you described."

He took in a deep breath, wanting very much to strangle his eldest brother. As the attendant returned with two of the priests and the globe of the oracle, Aeson crossed his arms over his chest.

The priest on the left bowed first. "Your majesty, you seek the Oracle's guidance?"

"No, follower of the path of the Epopisdeus," Kabril said. "My brother seeks its wisdom in regards to a mate."

The other priest gasped. "Such advice is frowned upon, my lord."

"Yet none of you hesitated to force my hand in finding a mate in that very fashion," Kabril reminded them. "You will do so for my brother."

"But, your majesty, what if the Oracle says he has no mate or that she once was but has perished?"

Aeson stiffened, his gaze locked on the white globe. He steeled his nerves and nodded. "Ask it. I wish to know regardless the outcome."

"Brother, you are certain?"

"Yes, Kabril. I am certain."

"Very well." His brother waved his hand dramatically in the air. "Priest, ask the Oracle."

The priests bent their heads, each humming and putting their hands over the globe. Aeson had seen it consulted enough to know no actual words were spoken. It was more a telepathic thing. The priests were seers—men able to connect with the oracle mystically.

The priest to the right turned his head towards Aeson. "It is most odd, my lord. The oracle tells us your mate is alive, but she will not be for long should you not find her."

His breath caught.

Kabril came up and off his throne, the smirk gone from his face. "What else does it say? Where is she? In what village does she reside? What does she look like? Her name?"

The priest to the left slumped his shoulders. "Your majesty, the Oracle responds in much the same way as when we ask it of other seers. It is vague. It is giving us only hints of it all, images, feelings, but they are short and incomplete."

"But that cannot be," Kabril said. "There are no female seers within our realm."

"Yes, there are none within our realm, your majesty, but legend speaks of seers born unto the human realm who are female."

Aeson still couldn't pull his mind from the knowledge his mate was alive but not for long.

His brother ran a hand through his hair, a nervous habit of his. "Aeson's mate is human?"

"Yes. It would appear so," a priest

answered.

The other tipped his head, as if listening to the Oracle. "Sparrow? It is showing us the image of a sparrow. This means something important. It is representative of her."

"But how is it she can be a shifter and born unto the humans?"

"Your majesty, it does not present the image in that of a shifter form. It is simply a sparrow. No more. No less."

Aeson grabbed for the priest. "Where do I find her? She needs me."

"My lord," the priest said, trying to free himself from Aeson's clutches. "Please, we know not."

"Brother." Kabril broke Aeson's hold on the priest. "Priests, is there anything more you can offer him?"

"It is strange. The Oracle wishes for him to go to where he has been drawn to so much as of late. We cannot say why."

Aeson's eyes widened. "It wishes me to go to the sex dungeon, erm, club in the human realm?"

Kabril rubbed the bridge of his nose

and the priests looked horrified at the idea of such a thing existing. "That is all. You may go."

They rushed off, taking the oracle with them.

"Brother, they are men who have dedicated themselves to the bird gods and who have forsaken carnal pleasures," Kabril said. "To talk of such a thing before them is unwise and cruel."

"And my mate is about to die," he answered. "I'll take the time to give a damn about the priests' celibacy when I know she is safe and well."

"I will gather men to accompany you," Kabril said.

Aeson shook his head. "This task is for me and me alone. Should I require assistance, I will send for it."

Kabril knew better than to argue the point. "Be well, brother, and may you find her healthy and eager to accept you."

CLICK TO BUY Master of the Hunt **today!**

About the Author

Dear Reader

Did you enjoy this title and want to know more about Mandy M. Roth, her pen names and all the titles she has available for purchase (over 100)?

About Mandy:

New York Times & *USA TODAY* Bestselling Author Mandy M. Roth is a selfproclaimed Goonie, loves 80s music and movies and wishes leg warmers would come back into fashion. She also thinks the movie The Breakfast Club should be mandatory viewing for...okay, everyone. When she's not dancing around her office to the sounds of the 80s or writing books, she can be found designing book covers for New York publishers, small presses, and indie authors.

Learn More:

To learn more about Mandy and her pen names, please visit www.MandyRoth.com

For latest news about Mandy's newest releases and sales subscribe to her newsletter: Sign Up For Mandy's Newsletter

Want to see all Mandy's books? Click here.

Printable PDF list of all Mandy's titles: Click here.

To join Mandy's Facebook Reader Group: The Roth Heads.

Review this title:

Please let others know if you enjoyed this title. Consider leaving an honest review on the vendor site in which you purchased this title. Reviews help to spread the word and boost overall sales. This means more books in the series you love.

Thank you!

facebook.com/AuthorMandyRoth

twitter.com/mandymroth

instagram.com/mandymroth

goodreads.com/mandymroth

pinterest.com/mandymroth

bookbub.com/authors/mandy-m-roth

youtube.com/mandyroth

amazon.com/author/mandyroth

Featured Titles from Mandy
M. Roth

The Immortal Ops Series World

Midnight Echoes

Isolated Maneuver

Expecting Darkness

Area of Influence

Act of Passion

Act of Brotherhood

Healing the Wolf

Wrecked Intel

And more to come…

Cozy Paranormal Mysteries

Once Hunted, Twice Shy

Total Eclipse of the Hunt

Don't Stop Bewitching

And more to come…

Tempting Fate Series

Loup Garou

Bad Moon Rising

And more to come…

The Guardians Series

The Guardians

Crossing Hudson

Ruling Jude

And more to come…

The Druid Series
Sacred Places
Goddess of the Grove
Winter Solstice
A Druid of Her Own
And more to come…

The King of Prey Series
King of Prey
A View to a Kill
Master of the Hunt
Rise of the King
Prince of Pleasure
Prince of Flight

Bureau of Paranormal Investigation (BPI)
Hunted Holiday
Heated Holiday

Prospect Springs Shifters
Blaze of Glory
Parker's Honor
Gabe's Fortune

CPSIA information can be obtained
at www.ICGtesting.com
Printed in the USA
LVOW10s1550230518
578229LV00001B/204/P